Books by R.D. Henham

RED DRAGON CODEX

BRONZE DRAGON CODEX

BLACK DRAGON CODEX

BRASS DRAGON CODEX
January 2009

GREEN DRAGON CODEX
June 2009

SILVER DRAGON CODEX
September 2009

WHITE DRAGON CODEX
January 2010

GOLD DRAGON CODEX
June 2010

BLUE DRAGON CODEX
September 2010

COPPER DRAGON CODEX
Spring 2011

BLACK
DRAGON CODEX

BLACK
DRAGON CODEX

R.D. Henham

MIRRORSTONE

Black Dragon Codex

Text by R.D. Henham with assistance from Ree Soesbee
Cover art by Vinod Rams
Interior art by Todd Lockwood
Cartography by Dennis Kauth
First Printing: September 2008

9 8 7 6 5 4 3 2 1

Library of Congress Cataloging-in-Publication Data

Henham, R. D.
    Black dragon codex / R.D. Henham.
        p. cm.
    Summary: When his mother is taken captive by an evil dragon lord, Septimus the black dragon and his human captive Satia, that was going to be his lunch, join forces to try and liberate his parent.
        ISBN 978-0-7869-4972-4
    [1. Dragons--Fiction. 2. Magic--Fiction. 3. Cooperativeness--Fiction.
4. Fantasy.] I. Title.
    PZ7.H3884Bl 2008
    [Fic]--dc22   2008013174

ISBN: 978-0-7869-4972-4
620-21777720-001-EN

U.S., CANADA,   EUROPEAN HEADQUARTERS
ASIA, PACIFIC, & LATIN AMERICA   Hasbro UK Ltd
Wizards of the Coast, Inc.   Caswell Way
P.O. Box 707   Newport, Gwent NP9 0YH
Renton, WA 98057-0707   GREAT BRITAIN
+1-800-324-6496   Save this address for your records.

Visit our Web site at www.mirrorstonebooks.com

Fought off by me and other heroes, Septimus flew back to his lair, snagging a young girl named Satia from the streets to have as a snack. It was then that an exciting adventure began—one involving unexpected transformations, unsavory red dragons led by a power-thirsty mage, and an unlikely alliance between a supposedly evil young dragon who longed to be considered an adult and that very same young girl who was meant to be his meal—

Oh, I must finish writing for now. That brass dragon is back with some story about a particularly interesting nest of giant centipedes he stumbled across. My notes on Septimus and Satia's tale are enclosed. I hope the stories of their adventure aid in your quest to learn more about the dragons of Krynn!

All my best,

Sindri Suncatcher

Distinguished Dragon Expert and
Expert at Distinguishing Dragons

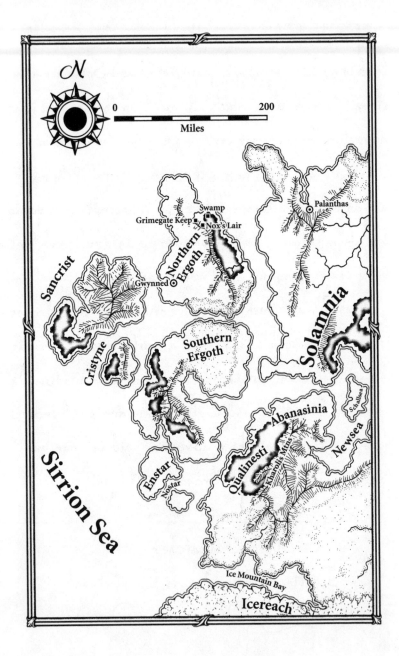

PROLOGUE

Septimus stretched his legs beneath the table, wishing once again that he could simply take to the sky and rain acid down over all these pale, scrawny, chittering two-legs. Not long now, he told himself. Not long at all, and his years of preparation, planning, and design would be over. He would have Gilean's Cup for his own, and he would be free.

It felt very strange to stand on long, thick legs, to feel the stubble of a beard on his chin. Even when he took human form through his magic, this wasn't the form he'd have chosen if it hadn't been necessary for the plan. It was too . . . *old*. But such things were necessary when one was dealing with arrogant, pig-headed humans who likened age and height to power. Septimus sighed. Humans were dumb. He didn't understand why Mother was so cautious of them.

On the stage, Withermyer the auctioneer spoke again. "The last item on our docket is Gilean's Cup. Bidding will begin in ten minutes. Gentlemen, please bring out the item." Although Withermyer kept talking, the buzz of the crowd quickly drowned him out. A few guards in gray, the color of the Underground thieves, lifted a large metal box up onto the platform. The preparations would clearly take a few more minutes, and the crowd already whispered in expectation.

Conversation buzzed around Septimus, but he hardly bothered to notice, speaking only when he was directly addressed. Instead, he reviewed his performance, his hands curling in his lap. The walk, perfect. The little habits, perfect. They had no reason to suspect that he was anything other than a kindly old man, no reason to think he'd like to tear out their throats and bathe in their blood. He had to shake his head to control himself, fight the instinctive, predatory urge. He wanted to attack, to roar, to strike out with his power and simply seize the prize!

"Gilean's Cup," he sighed, forcing the instincts down. "Chance of a lifetime." The humans around him nodded in agreement, babbling something in the incredibly simplistic language they used, the one he had learned in order to communicate with these prattling, chittering two-legs. He looked around the warehouse where the auction was being held, keeping a wary eye on his surroundings. Decorated with tapestries, chairs, and ornate candelabra, it passed as a well-to-do ballroom during the auction. Septimus didn't care about any of it—not the gilded candleholders, the silk and satin, not the jewels that shimmered on ladies' necks. Money was important to his hoard, but magic . . . ah, now that was worth risking his life to gain.

"How much—" a boy near him, tall and broad as an ox, began to ask. The boy's voice broke. The brown-haired human wall cleared his throat and tried again. "How much money do you think it will take to buy the chalice?"

Septimus studied the boy scornfully for a moment before he answered. Although Septimus wore the outer guise of an old man, he was actually quite close to the boy's age in relative years. Yet here this human, Rohawn, acted jittery and unsure, while Septimus had them all in the palm of his hand, just waiting for his opportunity to strike.

Was it true, then, that humans were a completely inferior race, suitable only as slaves and food? Or was it as his mother told him, that they were as dangerous as dragons with their magic and their cunning? Septimus felt a rush of excitement—here he was, standing among them in disguise. Not one of them had any idea. His guise was perfect. Even their leader, Elidor, seemed to have no idea that Septimus was anything other than what he seemed—a kindly old man with a great deal of money, willing to spend it all on a trinket that had caught his eye.

"Well, Diveena and I have pooled our resources, but I can only hope it will be enough," Septimus answered. "Our total comes to sixty-four thousand pieces of steel. I think we have a strong chance." Time was passing so slowly. Septimus could almost smell the magic of Gilean's Cup from across the room, and it felt like an eternity while the humans chattered, moving back and forth like ants through the warehouse ballroom.

At last, the bidding started. Septimus kept his hands folded in his lap so that no one could see his white-knuckled grip on his cane. The chalice was within his grasp. Undergoing this ruse of steel coins was only a formality. All that mattered was getting the chalice and taking it home so that he could, at last, prove himself. With a strong voice, Septimus tipped his hat to the crowd and bid a good portion of his money, but was then outbid. Back and forth he bid with the oily-haired elf across the room. Finally, though, he just bid all of his money, trusting to his human allies to support his final push for the cup.

"Sixty-one thousand two hundred pieces of steel, going once!" The auctioneer raised his gavel above the auction block. "Going twice!" Septimus smoothed his mustache, stepping toward the podium as though the prize were already his to claim. It was his. No one could take the magic chalice from him now—

"Sixty-one thousand," the elf's call came from the crowd. The auctioneer paused expectantly. The bid was not greater than Septimus's current price. A few giggles sparkled in the crowd as people waited to see if there would be an additional bid on top of the one that the elf called out.

Then a woman's voice, small and afraid, spoke out over the crowd. "I will add two thousand pieces of steel to Taliensier Orielesti's bid." All eyes turned to Diveena, who was standing alone at the back of the room in her simple black gown. She stared firmly at the ground, unable to look up and face the crowd. Septimus felt his stomach fall through to the floor.

"Diveena is bidding *against* Septimus!" someone exclaimed. She was his pawn—his ally! How could she do this to him?

"Going once!"

There was nothing Septimus could do. His last bid comprised all the steel he'd brought with him, the entirety of his barely begun hoard. It would have been enough, if he hadn't been betrayed in the end. *Humans!*

"Going twice!"

The rage Septimus felt could barely be suppressed. He gripped his cane until he could barely feel his hands. All the anger he'd bottled up while in disguise could not be controlled any longer.

"Sold!" cried the auctioneer, slamming the gavel down.

Septimus snapped the cane with an audible crack. He followed Diveena through the crowd to the door, where she was arguing with several of the humans he'd been befriending. "You did this to me. This is your fault, Diveena," he said, ignoring her protests. "After all my work. All my machinations. Everything ruined by the love of a foolish woman for a man who is too much an idiot to even realize it exists." The curly-haired human girl stepped in front of Diveena, and it was all Septimus could do not to throw her aside to get at his betrayer. "You've destroyed it all."

Diveena protested again, saying something about how she had to do it, but Septimus would have none of it. He'd done everything he knew to make the circumstances fall in his favor and get him the crystal chalice. "Weeks of work, destroying invitations so they would not be delivered," he listed. "The poison was so subtle that no one could trace it to me. I sabotaged three caravans to prevent patrons from having more money than I did at this auction, ensured shipments never made their destinations, made particular financial backers lose everything. I even hired brigands to comb the city for my targets, to steal money to add to my own. And you, with your foolish love, your useless human feeling—you've ruined it all."

"You did this?" The human boy, Rohawn, stared at Septimus in shock. "How could you hurt all those people?"

"That chalice is going to be the cornerstone of my hoard, you simpleton," Septimus snarled, hands still clenched around the ends of his broken cane. "And I'm not about to give it up so easily."

Across the room, the winning bidder stood on the stage beside the auctioneer. Septimus turned to face him, glaring over the heads of the applauding crowd toward the podium and the stage. All the indignities of forcing himself into this ridiculous human form came flooding back, all the slights he'd let slip by so that he could keep up the charade of his disguise. He *hated* acting human, hated pretending that he was anything less than the greatest predator on Krynn. And now, after all that, he'd lost the chalice to human treachery? Never.

"I will not be kept from my prize." Septimus dropped the two ends of the cane onto the floor angrily. "I am finished with this charade. Gilean's Cup is mine."

Before anyone could move, Septimus roared, a hollow, hideous sound that echoed as if they stood in a deep mountain cave. He swelled, his body doubling in size with every second. His fingers lengthened into claws, his neck elongated, growing wide, and thick scales bristled up from his spine. A tail lashed out behind him, tipped with a shining black wedge. Wings tore out from his back, spreading wide as he grew ever larger. The wings twisted in the curtains, ripping them down in long, fluttering shreds. No longer human in any way, Septimus the great black dragon roared again, snapping his jaws above the heads of the panicked crowd. "That cup is *mine!*" the dragon roared, his voice crashing like thunder. "And I will take it for my hoard!"

ou don't need me here. He's not going to die!" Satia pointed at her friend Kyran for emphasis, who lay sleeping on the bed recovering from the grave wound he'd received earlier that night. Now that the elf cleric who sat by the bed had recovered enough from her own sickness to heal Kyran, Satia's worry for him had abated and she worried more for the friends she'd so callously told off a few hours ago.

Sighing, the elf by the bed answered, "I know that. But we agreed that you should stay here and help me while the others went to the auction."

"Yes, we did. And it worked. He'll be fine." Grabbing her cloak, which had been dropped untidily on the floor by the inn room's door, Satia dragged it over her head and fastened the clasp. "I brought Kyran here so you could help him. Now that you've healed him, I know he'll be all right. I'll come back and visit him as soon as I'm done. You don't need anything else from me, and the others might. Who knows what might happen at that auction?" The elf sighed, but Satia bullied on. "I can help them."

"Satia," Kaja fixed the girl with a stern glare. "You must stay where it's safe. Kyran will wake up soon. Elidor and Rohawn and the others will have Gilean's Cup in no time. They don't need your help."

"Fine, fine." The girl sat down on a chair by the door, jerking her cloak off and crumpling it into her lap with a sigh. "I'll stay."

"You promise?"

"Kaja"—Satia put her chin in her hand, elbow on her knee—"would I fib to you?"

"Well . . . all right. I'll trust you." The cleric's demeanor softened into a smile. "You'll feel better knowing you did the right thing." She turned back to the wounded man, taking the towel from his head and dabbing it into a bowl of water. "I realize that you grew up here, and that you've spent a great deal of time down in those sewers with the thieves, but tonight you're safest—"

The soft bang of the door spoke volumes, and the cleric spun about to find an empty chair and the dying sound of feet rattling down the stairs and out the front door of the inn. The elf sighed. "Little liar."

The moon shone down, fighting through clouds to

peer down on the city. It was late night, a nip of chill coming in on the ocean's breeze, and the soft sound of church bells across the city echoed on stone and water alike. Satia darted from alley to alley, avoiding anyone walking the streets. Whether they were good people or bad, she didn't want anything to do with them. She didn't like people at all, really, unless those people were thieves.

Satia shimmied up a water pipe on the side of a building, made her way across the rooftops, and leaped nimbly from one to another where the buildings didn't adjoin. The thieves of Gwynned had given up long ago on following her during her nightly jaunts. Nobody could run the roofs like Satia, and she was the only one light enough to use the gutter pipes as ladders to the thin balconies high above the city streets.

"Got to catch up to them," she whispered after a particularly difficult leap left her scrabbling on the shingles of a warehouse roof. "If I don't get to the auction, those amateurs are all going to be in trouble. They don't know what they're doing—they're not even from Gwynned! How can they—"

Her inner monologue was cut off with a snap as a sudden sharp crack filled the night. It was followed by a bright flash and the echoing thunder of crumbling stone. Satia raised one hand to shield her eyes, recognizing in an instant the building where the explosion had occurred. "Oh no," she gasped. "That's where they were holding the auction!"

Pushing herself, Satia leaped to her feet and hurtled across the long warehouse roof, shingles flying out from under her feet. She didn't think about falling—nothing ever put her off balance—but imagining her friends in there, hurt, dying . . . Tears blurred her vision, and she pitched off the end of a building with both arms outspread, catching the edge of a balcony across the narrow alley. She locked her elbows around iron bars and pulled herself up. Across the street, the warehouse was crumbling, half in flames and half broken open like an eggshell. People were fleeing through the smoke into the streets.

Something roared within the flames, inexplicable and horrible. Satia saw a massive form rising from the smoke at the center of the building. It was large, four times the size of a horse, all bat wings and tail and lashing neck. A wedge-shaped head with eyes that drank the firelight twisted about on a scaled serpentine neck. The wings beat in an unbalanced rhythm, one slower than the other, causing the dragon to rise slowly amid the smoke and flame. His mouth was covered in some sort of goo that he was working to remove with his front paws as it flew.

Satia crawled onto the roof of the house across the street, facing the fire's roar, the heat fanning her cloak. Once the dragon got his mouth free, he roared even louder, and a horrible fear crept into her bones, sticking her feet to the roof as if glued there. Her jaw dropped. The dragon roared again, circling the building. A torn wing made his circle oblong, limping in the air until he paused right above her. Arrows shot past, missing them both by inches, but still the fear kept Satia from moving. A gust from his sweeping black wings tore away her cloak. It fluttered away, birdlike, to the ground. The dragon's head snaked back to glance at the ruined warehouse, to the streets where the city guard gathered archers to ready another barrage. The dragon hissed and spat acid on the cobblestone streets, scorching a long, virulent scar in the stone and scattering the archers.

The dragon seemed injured, his wing strokes laborious and uneven. It flew higher with an effort, roaring downward. It looked like it was searching for something. Letting out a roar of desperation and defeat, it rose into the air, leaving the building behind. Another screech, this one almost petulant, echoed from the gigantic lizard, but instead of growing smaller as it flew away, Satia stared at the black dragon as it grew larger. Who could have known she'd ever see a dragon this up close?

Blinking back to reality, Satia dodged and threw herself off the roof. Better to break a leg on the stone street three stories below than to be eaten by that tremendous monster. Her feet left the shingles, the wide gulf of space opening before her, but a shadow crossed her body—a shadow with steely, glinting claws. The dragon's claws snapped shut around her, and suddenly gravity reversed itself. Instead of the ground rising toward her, it began to fall away. Then the city shrank too, and then the island of Northern Ergoth, leaving nothing in Satia's sight but sky, clouds, and the dragon's iron grip.

Chapter Two

The ground rushed beneath Satia in a multicolored blur, like a quilt sliding off the bed. Satia had grown used to the feeling of huge, scaly claws wrapped tightly against her rib cage. Her panic hadn't lasted as long as the flight, fading into a thin, sheer terror that pulsed in her veins whenever the dragon took a particularly sharp turn. She didn't know where they were, or why, or where she was going to end up. All she knew is that she had one tiny steel dagger all the way down in her boot, and the dragon had twenty feet of thick, hard scale. When she tried to yell at the dragon and ask, it just ignored her. As they flew, she maneuvered herself in the dragon's claw to be able to reach her only weapon, puny though it might be.

It wasn't a particularly big dragon. When she twisted around to look up at it, she saw it was much smaller than she would have thought dragons were, really, and its wings would barely cover a small house.

Black scales covered thick muscles, and the long neck in front was balanced by a whiplike tail that lashed behind them in the wind. Its head wasn't as big as her body, so it would probably take it two or three bites to eat her. When it noticed Satia looking up at it, the dragon growled, and she saw sharp white teeth behind its snarling lips. It must be very young for a dragon. In fact, now that she was getting used to looking at it, the monster was really kind of puny, and—

A sudden, diving turn broke off her thoughts, and Satia's heart dived into her throat. Shrieking in sudden panic, she grasped the claws as hard as she could. Satia saw a low, bumpy mountain range spread below them that jutted up the center of a foul, horribly scented marsh. Thick willow trees and banyans strung together over high green grasses. Winding waterways covered the ground, and the foliage was so thick in places that she couldn't see even a speck of earth below. Cutting through that thick marsh on foot would take days or weeks—if it was even possible— but Satia soared above it all with a single stroke of the young dragon's wings, despite its erratic flight due to its injured wing. It seemed to have mostly recovered from whatever injury it had taken back at the warehouse, though there was a hesitation in its wingstrokes that made Satia think of a limp.

"Where are we going?" she screamed in useless frustration, banging her fists against the dragon's claws.

One of the mountains below them spiraled closer with each adjustment of the dragon's flight. Yet it still flew on, ignoring her yells. The mountain was larger than the rest, a great, bare, rocky head sticking up above the last sticky willow trees that ran along one side. It was one of the few dry spots within the damp, sludgy greenness. Squinting into the bright morning sun, Satia made out a patch of strangely shaped darkness under the rocks. That must be where the dragon lived, a cave just above the thick, gooey swamp. He was taking her home to eat her!

Satia screamed again as the dragon made a sudden dropping roll. The movement was far jerkier than their hours of calm flight, and Satia's ribs bruised in the creature's grip. Its thick, blocky head snaked out, and Satia could see what had attracted the massive creature's attention. There was a flood of smaller creatures buzzing about the opening of the cave. Flying people? Satia squinted. Hovering people, really, because they didn't seem to be flying all that well.

Standing in the opening of the cavern was another black dragon—and this one exactly matched the stories Satia'd heard. It was huge—easily five times the height and girth of the dragon carrying her—with wings that looked like they could blot out the sun. Satia could only imagine that the gliding creatures around it were human-sized, yet a single snap of the dragon's mouth could easily chomp two or three at once. Satia's jaw dropped along with her stomach—they were diving again, and this time rolling to the side to avoid a cluster of arrows. The dragon in the cavern's mouth roared and pawed at the flying things, its sharp claws ripping through one, causing the smaller pest to fall to the ground like a dropped stone.

Something burned past her cheek, and Satia raised one hand to touch her face. A single drop of acid had brushed against her from her captor's open maw. She screamed as she saw its neck convulse, then blast out thick, greenish fluid just a foot from her head. Once the panic left her—would it ever really leave?—she twisted in her narrow prison to see three armor-clad archers among the now sizzling trees, screaming in agony as the Black's acid washed over them.

But . . . did those archers have wings? The dragon's lips curled in a vicious smile, and land snapped past beneath Satia as it beat its wings to climb into the sky again. Tossed back and forth by the buffeting wind and shifting gravity, all Satia could do was hold on.

But as her captor gained altitude, she saw something even worse.

Two small red dragons, each perhaps half the size of the one holding her, dropped out of the cloud cover above, snaking forward on the wind with their wings unfurled. Her dragon ducked to avoid their dive, but a claw scored its mark across its black shoulder, and a gout of flame seared only a few feet from the leading edge of its wing. The fire stopped as quickly as it had come, the little red dragon coughing and choking in its own fumes. The second hissed at its companion, chastising it, and the first roared fussily and snorted out a double column of smoke from its nostrils. It might have been funny if Satia wasn't terrified.

The gigantic black dragon at the cavern caught sight of them, noting that the smaller black dragon was in trouble. With an earth-shaking roar, it leaped into the air, wings snapping out to knock aside many of the clustered flying creatures. Satia screamed as the other dragon rocketed upward far faster than she'd have expected, even though its wings and legs were thickly crusted with odd winged men . . . no, not men, Satia realized as they flew closer. Draconians.

Remembering the stories she'd heard about them—vicious, horrible lizard-men with strange magical powers—Satia clutched the black dragon's claws and prayed to Paladine that he wasn't going to put her down among them. She wasn't sure what would be worse: a relatively quick death in the dragon's jaws, or the slow torture of being cut apart by draconians. Then again, she realized as a sputtering gout of flame passed just beneath them, she *could* be burned alive.

The little black dragon carrying her was swerving to meet with the larger one, and the dragonfear emanating from that monstrous lizard cut through Satia's scream right to her heart. With every second it grew closer, Satia shivered. The draconians were screaming and shouting orders, plunging their spears into the big dragon's hide and watching the tips break off. Black blood trickled in rivulets of thick goo down the dragon's side as it snapped another of its tormentors in half. The body toppled from its jaws, turning to stone as it fell into the swamp. Satia shivered.

The faster of the young red dragons flashed past, trying another swoop with its claws, but the dragon holding Satia snapped a wing out and cracked the smaller Red across the jaw. The solid strike caused the Red to spiral, its eyes closing from the recoil. She was afraid for a moment that her captor might claw at its opponent, forgetting that it was still clutching her, but she didn't have to worry. The wing buffet had cost Satia's captor its balance, and the dragon tilted in the air. The second Red screamed in glee, pouncing forward to press the advantage—and that was when a tremendous shadow fell over them all.

The massive black dragon passed above them, but before it could spray out its acidic breath, a violent crackle broke through the screams of combat. Satia heard it and expected a thunderclap, but none came. Only a solitary bright bolt of lightning streaked against the clear blue sky. The bolt struck the larger dragon in the shoulder joint. The dragon shuddered as the lightning lanced through its body, and for an instant, Satia could see the outline of the dragon's skeleton beneath the thin leather of the wing. The smell of ozone and agony filled the air, and the dragon holding her roared in protest at the sight of the larger one shuddering in the sky.

The monstrous black dragon slowly regained its balance, its glistening ebony head whipping about in rage. Its wing beats were awkward now, its body trembling as it sought to keep altitude. As it lumbered in the sky, Satia could see beyond it, where the bolt came from. A man in strange, beautiful plate mail stood in the air—in the air!—beyond the large dragon. A clump of draconians surrounded him, struggling to glide awkwardly back and forth at his command. He had on a long golden cloak and armor glinting steel and ebony, the helm horned with vicious-looking antlers like those of a king stag. The man lifted his finger, cloak swirling, and chanted in a strange, echoing tongue.

Behind him, the twin red dragons swooped and cavorted like birds, nipping at one another like vicious puppies. The man in the steel armor ignored them, and they hissed and snarled, trying to churn up more fire in their bellies for another strike. Chanting, the wizard lifted his hands in the air again, and the twin red dragons snapped their heads forward eagerly to see what dangerous spell he would summon this time.

"Magic!" Satia pounded on her captor's claw. "Duck!"

Whether or not the dragon understood or even heard her, it tilted to the side. They spun end over end, the trees and mountains tilting crazily below. Sparks flew from the man's hand, arcing in a great electric cage that quickly surrounded the larger dragon. The massive black dragon roared, breaking partially free and trying to follow Satia's captor, but the cage closed, magical light sparkling around the Black's beating wings and flailing tail. The cage arced from one flashing spark to the next, linking everything together in a web of energy that surrounded the dragon. The Black spat viscous acid at its captors, but the chattering, laughing Reds ducked easily. The acid hit two of the draconians instead and they flailed about, spinning madly down in hissing, smoking trails. None of the spray reached the man in the golden cloak.

"Vex, Beset." The two young red dragons looked up with glittering eyes at the floating wizard, hanging on his every word. "Get the little one. He'll help us ensure the mother works for our noble cause."

The twin reds roared gleefully and rushed toward the young Black and its captive, wings straining with each maneuver. Satia's captor righted himself, roaring madly. With a wild burst of power in his wings, he pounded back toward the draconians thrusting spears into the captive dragon's ribs. The man with the golden cloak turned in the air, his movements light and graceful, and Satia sensed he was laughing beneath his golden helm. Draconians split off from the main force, swooping toward them on outstretched, brassy wings. Their horrible, lizardlike faces snarled, drool flying from their bared fangs, and clawed hands clutched at metal-tipped spears. The young black dragon paused, still roaring, wings beating madly as the Reds came closer with each second.

"No! Don't go back there! They'll catch us too!" She could hardly believe she was saying it. Help the dragon who brought her so far from Gwynned, probably just to eat her? Still, those spears were sharp, and the draconians looked as if they'd enjoy pulling her apart bit by bit. "Get out of here!"

But the little dragon raged forward, backing down only when the larger black dragon roared commandingly.

The wizard snarled again and the draconians redoubled their speed. They were a little bigger than humans, their bodies thicker, tails jutting out from beneath thick leather armor. Their wings beat heavily in the air, and their flight was awkward, more of a glide than truly flying. It seemed for a moment that the little black dragon would get away, but then another cascading shower of sparks surrounded him, threatening to trap him as it had trapped the larger dragon.

Satia's hair stood upright within the energy field, and their bodies jerked to a halt as they were held aloft not by the dragon's beating wings, but by the magic of the net. Her body spasmed as pain lanced in her bones, through her muscles, in every breath. The dragon quaked as though he, too, felt pain. He hissed and spat acid, and the draconians had to swoop in wide circles to avoid the worst of it, their stubby wings incapable of more elegant maneuvering.

Satia looked down as she was tossed back and forth and saw the tops of the willow trees waving below her feet, almost close enough to reach past the bars of the energy cage. As she struggled, desperate to be free of the dragon's claws, her hand flew open and dropped the steel dagger she'd been clinging to. It spun down in jerky arcs, passing through the beams of the energy cage and vanishing between the branches below. Satia gasped. The cage was wide, shaped to hold a dragon—not a human. If she could get free of the dragon's grasp, she could fall through the cracks—just like the knife! It would be a long fall, but the ground below was spongy and damp. She could make it! Satia writhed, feeling the small black dragon's grasp loosening as pain shot through them both again. Just a little more . . .

Suddenly the air around her felt tight and strange. She looked up at the golden-cloaked man hovering near the larger cage, then saw the tremendous, horrible black dragon at a distance opening her mouth to speak strange, echoing words like the ones that had formed the cages. Dragon magic?

The claws around her waist shrank, altered by magic. The black scales paled, merging into skin, the arm suddenly pulling into itself by the power of the other dragon's spell. Satia screamed as the force holding her up vanished. She caught a glimpse of a roaring head, the skull changing, compressing to the size of her own, the obsidian eyes narrowing and becoming less skull-like, and hair springing from the place that long dragon horns had once curled around the forehead. The roar became a scream that matched her own, and Satia found herself tumbling out of the sky, through the bars of the energy cage toward the willow trees below.

At her side was a young boy, just a few years younger than she was, his surprised eyes meeting hers with a horrified gaze. They twisted in the air, the blue sky vanishing between the branches as they plunged down through the treetops. Her own scream was drowned out by the boy's panicked cry.

"MAMA! NO!"

CHAPTER THREE

Satia searched around, crawling through the underbrush. Every bone in her body ached, and she could
swear she hadn't missed a single tree branch on the way
down. Any minute now, those draconians would return,
swooping through the marshes to find them. She had to
get out of here, but rushing into the swamp unarmed
was as much a death sentence as staying here.

There was a rustle beneath a half-fallen willow,
and a young boy crawled out. He looked about ten,
just younger than she was, and his hair was short,
spiky, and jet black. Tears streaked his pale, angry face,
making the too-black eyes strange and liquid. It was the
dragon that had been carrying her—but he was a person
now. A human, she thought specifically, wearing dark
clothing—a simple tunic and leather trousers, much
like her own. For a moment, Satia glared at him, and
he returned the look with poison. She turned back to
the earth, scrambling around.

"Mama!" screamed the boy, looking up through the trees and bouncing on the balls of his feet while his arms scrabbled at the air. "Mama!"

Terrified that his cries would bring the draconians, Satia spun and tackled the boy, shoving one hand over his mouth. "Be quiet! They'll find us!"

He struggled against her, and she could make out his words, even muffled as they were beneath her hand. "That's my mother they've got up there! I have to help her!"

"What are you going to do?" Satia jibed cruelly. "Fly up there on your scrawny arms and bite them with your great big teeth?" When he paused, shocked at her tone, Satia let him go and backed away. "If you want to run after those draconians, you go right ahead. Can you turn back into a dragon?"

The boy shook his head. "I tried," he said sullenly. "But I'm not the one who turned me into a human. My mother did it. I was a human in Gwynned by my own power, so I could turn back whenever I wanted. This spell isn't my own—so I can't control it." He peered up through the thick underbrush, falling suddenly silent. Satia heard the sweep of wings above, somewhere just above the thick willow canopy. The two stood perfectly still as the sound crept past and then vanished deeper into the bog.

Satia went back to rooting around under the trees, running her hands through the thick, still waters of the bog.

"What are you doing?" asked the boy.

"Finding my knife," she replied. "Once I find it, I can start making my way back to Gwynned."

"You'll never make it."

"Yeah? And you'll never find your mom. I guess we're both sunk." Satia snarled out the words without thinking, but once they came out of her mouth, the thought actually sank in. They *were* sunk. She had no idea where Gwynned was from here, much less how she was going to travel that far, alone, across the wilderness. Something large swooped past overhead, close enough to cause the top branches of the trees to waver slightly. One of the red dragons? Satia and the boy both froze, and it moved on.

The boy paced through the underbrush. His movements were lithe, feral, and graceful. She could all but see the dragon in him, moving predatorily toward her. His eyes fixed on hers with the blank, unblinking glare of a serpent. "I can do this. If I can infiltrate humans for a month, go to an auction and nearly steal one of the most powerful magic items on Krynn, then I can save my mother too."

"Nearly?" Satia jibed halfheartedly.

He ignored her, brow furrowed in thought. "I had years to make that plan, to create a persona, to memorize how you humans act, learn your language, be perfect in my disguise. There's no time to do all that planning now. I have to think of something to help my mother—and fast." He cast his gaze around frantically, trying to pull himself together, and his eyes fell on Satia. "You. You'll help me get my mother back." Something in the way he said it made Satia's heart catch in her throat. She froze, expecting some magical effect.

Nothing.

"No." Satia went back to looking for her knife.

He blinked, stunned. "No?" His eyes narrowed and he stiffened, clenching his hands into fists and glaring at her again. "I order you to help me get my mother back!"

"I already told you—no." She turned and went back to digging through the muck, scurrying around a tree to check the puddles on the other side.

"But . . . I used dragon magic on you. You *have* to do it."

"I guess it didn't work." She shrugged.

His jaw dropped. For a moment, the boy looked so lost and vulnerable that Satia almost forgot he was a horrible, murderous dragon. He looked down at his hands, trying to clench them into claws—but they were still fingers. He studied his arms, poking at the skin as if expecting black scales to appear. Finally, he sank to the ground in the middle of the clearing, hiding his head in his crossed arms.

"Look, kid . . ."—Satia paused, her arms covered to the elbow in muck—"you need to be thinking about how you're going to get out of here." She couldn't help continuing nervously, "You also need to think about the fact that you are going to be in a lot of trouble for kidnapping me. My father's . . . uh . . . the Prince of Gwynned! And he'll send troops and . . . soldiers . . . and stuff after me."

Innocent of the ways of humans, he believed her, but that still didn't help. "It doesn't matter. It will take them months to get here through the bog." The boy rubbed at his eyes. "Anyway, you're stuck here, just like me. I can't leave. Not while he's got my mother."

Cursing inwardly that her lovely lie hadn't gotten the reaction she wanted, Satia asked through gritted teeth, "Who?"

"Thordane. The wizard.'"

Satia narrowed her eyes. "You knew that guy up there?"

"Sort of."

He let out a little hiccup, and Satia realized he

was crying. She crawled over to him and awkwardly patted his shoulder. "Um . . . look. If you want, you could come with me . . ." It really felt odd, she had to admit, feeling sorry for someone who'd been planning to eat her not a candlemark ago.

"I can't leave her. He's going to make her his mount!" the boy raged, pounding the marshy ground with a fist. "He's going to make her a slave."

That caught Satia's attention. Slavery wasn't uncommon in Gwynned. She'd seen the men and women unloaded off the boats in chains, sold, and dragged off to who knows where, the glimmer in their eyes slowly fading as the years passed. She'd even known a slave when she was a child. He'd played catch with her in the back alleys while he washed his master's laundry. Once, they caught him at it and accused him of shirking his tasks. He'd been given twenty lashes and hung in the street all day long for passersby to mock. They never played catch again.

"My name is Septimus," the boy said, and she blinked out of the memory. "Septimus. The old man. Remember?"

She blinked. "You were the old guy with the cane?"

"It took me two years to get my face right," the boy mourned. "I studied how to walk on two legs, how to brush my hair and wash my skin without shredding it—you're so fragile! I memorized about eighty different ways to tell kids to stop playing in the street, just to help the disguise. I even saved up a lot of steel pieces so I could buy it outright, because Mom said that was safer than just barging into the city and killing everyone," he said matter-of-factly. "Not that any of my hard work helps now."

"Wow. Why was it so important to infiltrate the city?" Satia asked, impressed.

He hung his head. "I was in Gwynned trying to find a magic item for my hoard."

"Your what?" she asked quizzically.

"My hoard! My treasure hoard. Until I have a magic item to start the hoard, I can't move out and make my own way in the world. It's a rite of passage." He stared at her as if she were a foreign plant. "You humans are so primitive."

"Hey!" She jabbed him. "You're human now too, you know!"

"Not for long," he snarled, eyes thinning to cresents. "All I have to do is free my mother, and she'll turn me into a dragon again and everything will be fine."

"Wait, wait. I thought dragons were used to being people's mounts. All the Dragon Highlords . . ."

He spun on her quicker than a striking snake.

33

"The Dragon Highlords worked for Takhisis! They were chosen by a goddess! The dragons worked with them, not for them!"

She hushed him, but his words echoed through the marsh, louder than the burbling brooks and *futt-futt-futting* gas bubbles of the deeper water. Satia stared upward in fear, desperately trying to sense whether the boy's cry had alerted the draconians, but she didn't hear the sound of leathery wings overhead.

"Nevertheless," she said, "we have to move. Those draconians will be back, and if they heard you yelling, they'll have a pretty good idea where we are." Satia scrambled to her feet.

"Listen to me, human. I may still be young among my kind," Septimus said haughtily, "but I'm more than a century old. I know things."

"Oh yeah? Like what?"

He grinned, and at this close distance she could see that his otherwise perfect human visage was completely spoiled by the sharply pointed tips of his teeth. "Like, I know where Gwynned is. And if I can fly, I can get you there. Back to your father, the prince." By Paladine, this kid was a sucker. "Let's make a trade: you help me free my mother, and I'll take you home—unharmed." He paused and then stuck out his hand. "I'll even give you my word on it."

Satia considered him, looking the boy-dragon up and down with all the street wit she could muster. Was he lying? He didn't show any of the signs of it—he wasn't sweating, he stared her right in the eye, he didn't shift from foot to foot. But then again, did dragons do any of those things when they were lying? Maybe they swished their tail or something. "How can I trust your word?" Satia asked slowly, not wanting to insult him. After all, she'd just seen him cry. "You're an *evil* dragon."

"I may be evil"—the boy looked at her from under furrowed brows—"but I can be bargained with." He paused, trying to think of something. Finally he ventured, "I'll swear by Takhisis?"

"Ew, no." Satia wrinkled up her nose.

"Yes, probably a bad idea. My mother didn't fight for her in the war, so the goddess probably wouldn't hold me to the promise anyway." He pondered, looking abashed, his hand still sticking out.

Satia grabbed it and shook. "I accept."

"What?"

"Your mother didn't fight for Takhisis? She wasn't involved in stealing the dragon eggs to make *them*." Satia pointed upward nervously at the draconians. "Your mother kept the peace between the dragons, when the others stole eggs, and lied, and broke their

35

promises. That tells me your word still means something. I'll help you—your mother in exchange for my freedom and a ride home."

"It's a deal." They grinned at one another, and then ducked as the swoop of wings overhead brushed against a willow tree. For a long moment, the two children huddled against the roots of the wide-bodied tree. The wings flapped lazily about, and Satia could imagine the stubby muzzle of the brassy orange creature sniffing around among the leaves. A few minutes later, he flapped away, but they could hear him yelling in a high-pitched, wheedling tone. "He's calling for his friends," Septimus whispered.

"You can understand him?"

He rolled his eyes. "He's speaking Draconic."

"Fair point." Satia scrambled out from under the tree roots. "Let's go. We were pretty far from your mother's cave when we fell, and I think Thordane was headed west. I saw a castle over that way when we were flying past, right on the edge of the swamp. If we're careful, we can get there by nightfall." Satia grinned and pushed into the underbrush, feeling the sludgy swamp give way under her feet. Well, if mud-filled boots was the worst thing in store for them in this marsh, she was probably lucky. Well, partially lucky. After all, she still hadn't found her knife.

Septimus reached up curiously and pulled a thin steel dagger from a crook in the tree roots. "Hey, Satia," he called out softly as he trotted after her. "Is this yours?"

CHAPTER FOUR

She should have seen it coming, sensed that they were being watched. Three days of marching through the swamp with Septimus, with no food other than a few berries and roots and next to no sleep, had dulled her senses. But still, she should have heard the movement!

They'd gotten tired and started walking on dry ground. In the marsh, that was as good as a beaten path, but she should have known that path would be watched. The sword hissed from out of nowhere, slicing past Satia's ear with barely an inch to spare. Satia cursed and threw herself to the ground away from the shimmering draconian that dropped out of the tree right beside her. She rolled through the sludgy terrain and scrambled for her knife. They were close to the fort she'd seen from the air. Of course Thordane had set guards!

Satia managed to raise her dagger to parry the

38

draconian's next swing. The creature's attack was so fierce that it sent shivers up her arm to her elbow. Raising the weapon again, the draconian sneered over her and flicked its long tongue against her cheek. Before it could bring the blade down, there was a roar to one side, and Satia saw a fully extended body fly overhead, colliding with the draconian headfirst and knocking it to the side. Septimus.

She'd hit her head on the way down, and Satia shook it carefully, trying to rattle her thoughts back into place. They were still in the swamp, on a low grassy knoll that jutted out through the sludgy water. Moss and wet grasses squished beneath Satia's elbow when she pushed herself up, trying to see what was going on.

The fight had rolled down the hill into the shallow bog water. The young boy—no, young dragon—clawed and kicked ferociously at the larger draconian, ignoring the sword in the creature's hand. The draconian cried out, unable to stab the boy, who simply wouldn't let go. He clawed at the creature's muzzle, digging his fingers into the beast's eyes as it flailed about beneath him. Satia scrambled to her feet, the sheer ferocity of Septimus's feral attack startling her. It was so horrifying that she almost missed the second draconian's thrust from behind.

As she jumped, the sword skidded along her side, burning her ribs like a hot brand. Satia stabbed in return, her short dagger sticking for a moment in the draconian's leather breastplate. She jerked the knife back out, and the horrible creature laughed. She was just going to have to trust that Septimus would be all right.

The creature fighting her had a squat, thick muzzle on a lizardlike skull, its grinning leer revealing thick, pointed teeth. A forked tongue flashed out excitedly. Reddish, metallic, snakelike scales flexed and rippled over ropy muscles.

"Thessse are the onesss," hissed the draconian as it closed in on her. "Take the boy alive—we need him as a hostage. The girl isss just a lucky bonus."

The other draconian managed to roll out from under Septimus, using the boy's light weight against him and pitching Septimus through the air. Satia saw Septimus on all fours in the water, grinning, teeth white against the dark mud splattered on his skin. The draconian, clearly unused to taking prisoners, advanced cautiously. Septimus, on the other hand, lunged forward again with his fingers splayed like claws and his teeth snapping. Satia could have sworn she saw him spit on the draconian before he slammed into it again.

"Septimus!" she called. "You're a person now!

Fight like people!" Apparently, in all of his studying humans to infiltrate them, he hadn't studied how they fight. Then again, Satia thought grudgingly, he probably hadn't needed to learn that for his trip to Gwynned, as he could have turned back into a dragon at any time.

Still, he sunk his teeth into the draconian's shoulder and ignored her cries.

Satia's opponent fumbled at its belt, pulling up a horn that hung on a leather lanyard. Realizing that it was about to call for help, signaling their location, Satia followed Septimus's lead and hurled herself on her enemy, stabbing her short dagger into the creature's arm. The draconian yelped loudly and dropped the horn, then swiped at her again with its sword. Old reflexes long honed by a lifetime in the streets of Gwynned took over, helping Satia dodge in and out of the draconian's reach. It was almost fun, watching the slower draconian try to keep up with her. It would never have made it on the Underground, the thieves' road in Gwynned.

Satia scored another hit on the draconian, carving a bloody line down the creature's arm. It roared and swung its thick short sword wildly, but Satia darted in with her back against the creature's stomach. Elbow to the belly under the breastplate, fist to the face—a punch that knocked three teeth loose—and then a vicious stomp on the creature's instep. As the draconian howled in rage, Satia grabbed its sword out of its fist and spun around to face it. With a cruel, desperate double thrust, Satia plunged both sword and dagger forward, under the creature's armor and into its belly.

The monster roared, but the cry was cut off sharply as a horrible crackling filled the air. The draconian's skin lost its red color, turning gray and dense. Its face stiffened, mouth half open, a rocky veneer crawling lickety-split over every inch of its hide. All motion stiffened. The creature's movements slowed, and then halted entirely with a horrible creak of granite and slate. Finally, the draconian stopped moving altogether, turning entirely to stone.

Surprised, Satia tried to jump back, but found her weapons frozen solid within the creature's stone belly. Like a statue formed around the blades, the draconian's dead form was solid and unyielding. Satia had no choice but to give up the weapons—or remain stuck with them.

Satia ducked under the stone draconian's upraised arm, looking around for Septimus and the second draconian. She found them thrashing about in foot-deep black water. The draconian's sword had been lost in the scuffle, probably dunked somewhere under the water, and Septimus showed the marks of multiple vicious bites and claws all over his arms and shoulders. His opponent had taken similar wounds, but Septimus's clawless hands and smaller teeth had done little more than anger his opponent. It was definitely an uneven fight. But it would be fairer once it was two to one.

Satia charged down the little knoll into the water. "Take that!" She thrust out her fist, cracking the draconian in the jaw. "Ow!" she cried, her fist stinging. "Ow, ow!" Satia hopped up and down, shaking her hand as the draconian advanced.

Luckily, Septimus followed her strike with a savage bite to the draconian's forearm, and the creature shrieked in pain. Septimus's weight overbalanced the draconian, and it fell to the marshy ground.

"What do you want with us?" Satia didn't punch the draconian again. Instead, she jumped on its chest to help Septimus keep it down. Their enemy flailed about in the water, desperately seeking its sword, but its hand came up filled with muck and kelpy goo.

"Thordane commands that we bring the boy to the keep," the draconian hissed, still struggling, but weaker now. "He is necessary to make Nox obey."

"Nox?" Satia cocked her head.

"He's talking about Mum," Septimus said through clenched teeth. With a growl, he grabbed a handful of mud and ground it into the draconian's face, watching as the creature spat and writhed.

Sighing, Satia grabbed the draconian's breastplate and asked, "Where are they holding the dr— uh . . . Nox?"

"In the heart of the keep. In the Great Hall," choked the draconian. "We told her that we already had the boy. We'd kill him if she didn't obey Thordane's orders." It sank its claws into Septimus's arms, drawing four thick lines of blood on the pale skin.

"You're blackmailing my mother?!" shrieked Septimus.

"Septimus, calm down. We have to ask more questions!"

"There's nothing else I want to know." Septimus allowed Satia to push him away as the monster sat up. Quickly, Satia grabbed the draconian by the shoulders and started undoing the straps of its breastplate. There was enough leather here to tie its wrists, maybe even its ankles. Satia tugged off the creature's upper armor and started jerking off the straps while the creature scrabbled the mud off its face.

Suddenly, a bright blade sprouted from the draconian's chest, plunging forward from the rear. There was the thick, hard sound of another shove, and the monster gasped, scrabbling at the steel that sprouted through its chest. Its fingers stiffened, red-orange skin losing its color and turning a rough gray. In seconds, this one, too, had turned to granite. Enraged, Septimus tried to jerk the sword out, snapping the hilt from the blade.

Satia spun as Septimus released the sword. "Why did you do that?" she cried. "It was our prisoner. It could have told us things—"

"It'd already told me everything I need to know. My mother is in that keep. She's being blackmailed. She thinks they've caught me." The small boy stared at her, black eyes unblinking. "She'll do what they say. My mother loves me."

Caught completely off guard by his merciless ferocity, Satia could do nothing but stare. The idea of an evil dragon loving anything was puzzling to her. Floundering for words, she shrieked, "You can't just kill someone like that!"

On the knoll, the other draconian's body suddenly creaked, cracks running sharply down the stone surface. In seconds, the entire draconian statue crumbled to pieces of stone and then to dust. The blades Satia had used to kill it fell at Septimus's feet. He looked at them, then looked at her. "Why not? You did."

"What I did was different. It was trying to kill me."

"So was that one," Septimus pointed at the still-rocky corpse. "Do you think that just because it was helpless for a few moments it was any less dangerous?"

"That's not the point. Killing is wrong. You may have pretended to be a human in Gwynned, but you certainly didn't understand what we're all about if you never learned *that* lesson."

Septimus stared at her silently. The words hung in the air, stale and empty.

Satia frowned. "Look, killing in self-defense is one thing, but if there's any other way to stop a fight, that's better." Seeing that Septimus disagreed, Satia put her hands on her hips. "Otherwise, our deal is off." Her voice was a low, dark threat.

Septimus stiffened, considering. At last, he snorted a gust of air from his nostrils. "All right."

"Good." Satia reached down and picked up her dagger, stuffing it back in her boot. The short sword she weighed in her hand a moment, considering the light blade. "This is good workmanship. Too bad you broke the other one. You could have used it instead of your hands." But then again, considering the look that Septimus shot her after that, maybe she didn't want him to have any kind of weapon at all. "They're at the keep. At least we're sure of that now."

Her companion stared darkly at her. "We know one more thing."

"What's that?"

In the bog, the second draconian cracked and crumbled, falling apart piece by piece as the rigor of its death wore off. Within the space of a breath, the creature's dust was swallowed by the black waters of the swamp.

"They can die," Septimus said evenly, "just like everybody else."

CHAPTER FIVE

"W hat is that smell?" Satia pinched her nose, clambering along through the rolling marshy hills. They'd climbed above the watery bracken, pushing their way up onto sludgy hills. Bigger mountains poked up their heads here and there in the distance, overlooking this lumpy, wet area. Over the hill ahead of them, they could see the rocky parapets of the keep that Satia had noticed from above.

"Marsh mud." Septimus reached back to pull her up by the hand over a fallen, mossy tree. "The deep kind."

"Deep kind?"

"Yeah, the kind you dig up from underground. It's been beneath the surface of the water, trapped between layers of stone, mixed with corpses of . . . well . . . everything that ever died in the bog." His expression was matter-of-fact, completely unaffected by the bitter, cloying smell. "These are the Mudcliff Crags. That fort you saw is held by ogres. I remember my mother telling me about it." His voice fell silent at the mention of his mother, and Septimus let go of Satia's hand. Turning and snarling, he slid onto his belly and wiggled up the rest of the hill, looking over the ledge. Satia followed him, eager for a first look at the crags.

"Well, I know a lot about swamps too." Satia swallowed, trying to sound confident. Septimus just stared at her. "They have . . . swamps near Gwynned. Outside the city. Down the beach. It gets . . . marshy . . . sometimes. Really squishy and wet and stuff." Realizing that this lie wasn't going over as well as the earlier one about her father, Satia fell silent under the cold stare of Septimus's dark eyes.

The area below them was just as lumpy and wet as the lands they'd traveled through, but here the mountains came together into a half bowl, arching from north to south along the eastern rim of the encampment. The fort stood against one of the cliffs, leaning drunkenly against the mountain. Its walls were carved from dark stone blocks chopped from the mountainside, mortared together with black mud that had long ago turned solid. The years had not been kind to this old keep, and the wear and tear of marshy weather showed on its pitted stone. Two lumbering towers jutted up on either side, one stiff and straight, the other cocked at an angle, buttressed up against a ledge high along the mountain wall. The keep itself was splattered between these two guardians at the end of a pebbled road that ran along the lip of a deep stone quarry.

Small figures carrying big wicker baskets trudged around inside the quarry. There was a faint booming sound, and a shelf of mud slid down the side of the quarry in a long, melting pile, like a slow-motion avalanche. The little figures hurried forward to collect the mud into their baskets. At this distance, Satia had to squint to make out the greenish color of their skin under the thick crusting of black mud. Larger forms wearing piecemeal metal and leather armor marched around the quarry, inside and on top, cracking long whips of rawhide. From here, Satia could also see that part of the keep's roof had collapsed long ago, leaving a portion of the keep open to the air. "That's how they got Nox . . . your mother . . . in. The red dragons probably live in there too." She pondered, quick eyes taking in every detail. Several draconians circled above the opening like crows, lowering themselves into the keep or lifting off from it in order to go about their business in the quarry or the swamp.

"There's a work camp down by the road." Septimus pointed with a black fingernail. "The buildings are all made of junk. Probably goblin made." Satia looked where he indicated and saw five ramshackle buildings of wood surrounded by a number of tents, stationary wagons, and a small corral of horses. "Workers, I guess, for the quarry."

"I don't think the goblins live in those buildings, though. I only see big things. Humans, maybe."

"Or hobgoblins. They're too small to be ogres," Septimus agreed. "It looks like the goblins live in there." He gestured again, and Satia picked out a portcullis against the lower levels of the keep. A well-packed dirt road wound down from the portcullis into the deep stone pit.

Two guards stood watch over the portcullis as much smaller figures trudged in and out of the keep. "The goblins are slaves?" she asked.

"Looks like it."

"Well, if there are humans in that work camp, then we might not be noticed if we snoop around a bit. The camp is large enough that we can keep hidden and still overhear conversations. Maybe those hobgoblins will mention something we can use." She pushed back a lock of curly black hair, twisting it angrily around her finger. "You speak Goblin, right?"

He favored her with a withering stare. "They'll be speaking Common."

"How do you know that? Some kind of dragon mind control?"

Septimus scowled. "I told you. All of my dragon powers went away when my mother turned me into this pathetic little human form. If I'd done it with my own spell—like the one I used in Gwynned—I'd still have all my powers. That's the difference between a spell that lets you change yourself, and a spell that forces a change on someone else. The first one is a disguise. The second"—Septimus flexed his hand into a small fist—"is a prison."

"So you looked like an old man in Gwynned—"

"Because then people would treat me with respect, yes. I was there to get the chalice for my hoard, so I needed people to think of me as something other than a boy." His face fell into hard lines. It looked strange on the boy's cherubic features. "Humans treat their young like invalids."

Satia slid away from the edge of the hill, nodding. "Yes." She remembered the cleric back at the inn who refused to let her go help her friends. A bitter wave of anger swept over her at the memory. If she'd just been there to help them . . . "I know. But you still didn't answer my question. How do you know that the hobgoblins speak Common?"

"Because if they work for the human, he'll make them," Septimus said with a sneer. "My mother didn't want me to go to Gwynned. She said I wouldn't find anything, and that if I were discovered, the humans would attack me. I didn't believe her. I didn't think any human would be able to best a dragon, even one as young as me. But now look what happened. One of them got *her*. For all her warnings, everything she told me to watch out for, one of your kind's taken her prisoner." Septimus met Satia's eyes. "I guess she was right. Humans are dangerous."

"You better believe it," Satia grinned. "So it's a good thing you've got one on your side too."

Septimus gave a slow, surprised blink, and then matched her smile. "Yeah. I guess it is."

To call it a village would have been insulting to villages across Krynn. "Refugee camp" was closer, but the five buildings that had been erected on the muddy earth were far too solid to be temporary. Tents were pitched hibberty-gibberty about, just enough to keep the rain off snoring heads, but the majority of the populace clambered in and out of the biggest of the buildings, the one with a painting on the door that looked like a mug made out of a grinning skull. Satia had to give the artist credit—it was a very good rendition. Then again, whoever painted it had probably drunk foaming bitter ale from a skull, so they had a lot to go on to make it look real.

The two of them crept through the town at dusk, using the long shadows and growing darkness to hide their approach. Hobgoblins had excellent night vision, but that time between night and day, the mix of glare from the setting sun and long shadow brought on by night baffled their sharp eyes. Or so Septimus said—and Satia had no reason to doubt him. They crept between tents, ducking behind barrels, their feet sinking deep in the gripping mud. Once, they had to dart into a tent, hoping against hope that it was empty, while three burly hobgoblins in plate armor and leather tromped by, arguing about a debt.

At last, Septimus and Satia hunched down behind a rain barrel under the sloping eaves of the pub, crouching tightly against the wall of the building and listening to the conversations inside. There was a lot of bragging, a lot of yelling, and the occasional shout of a fist fight. "We'll be safe here," Satia said.

"You sure?" Septimus glanced around warily, pressing his back to the wall.

"Oh, yes. I use this tactic a lot. People always look out the window. They never look down." Satia grinned.

Septimus responded warily, "You learned that being a princess in Gwynned?"

Satia's face fell. "Well . . . maybe I exaggerated about my father—" Before she could continue, a loud bark of laughter in the inn drowned out anything else she might have said.

". . . and so I were tellin' him, that ain't no way to treat yer gobbos! Ya gots to beat goblins till their ears start workin'—then they'll listen to ya." The first voice rumbled like it came from a big belly full of ale.

"Half those gobbos wouldn't listen even if you beat 'em with their own mother's ears! They're only there to serve their time and get out." The second voice, sharp as iron knives, laughed as it talked. The sound grated on Satia's nerves.

"Yeh! But their time gonna be forever! They ain't never going to fix up that much money—not when they don't even get paid!" The first guffawed. "Holg's got a heck of a system worked out. Them gobbos'll be working forever for scraps, and we'll be living high on the hog!"

Talking through a mouthful of—well, of something Satia didn't want to know about—the second agreed. "Minin' mud. Who would've thought it'd make so much steel?"

"Don't complain. We gots good mortar, good brick-work, good for packin' roads. We gots a way around the dangerous mud slides by using goblins—so nobody cares if'n they die. Think about it, Dugadee, it's a good life! Ain't much glory in it, but a heck of a lot of money. The Highlord of Dirt, he knows his stuff, makin' them gobbos grub about in the mud so we all get rich."

Satia couldn't help it. She leaned forward a bit, peering upward to see them through the slant of the window. The two hobgoblins were so engrossed in their conversation that they didn't notice her, but she got a good look at them. The first was short and stocky, muscles rippling under blubbery layers of fat, but his beady eyes were quick and sharp.

The second hobgoblin lowered his voice, leaning forward over their table, and his horrible pockmarked green face turned paler beneath the mud-crusted shock of wiry black hair as he spoke. "Best not talk that way, Urgo, not when one of these boys could take it to the baaz working for Thordane." His watery red eyes darted back and forth in the crowded pub, looking for eavesdroppers everywhere but beneath the window-sill. "Now that he's got a dragon working for him, we best keep our voices down. If'n there's a problem, he'll send the ogres. Or worse, the baaz. You want that kind of trouble?"

The other hobgoblin lowered his voice grumpily. "Dragon don't work for him yet. If she knew we really didn't have her kid under wraps—"

"But she don't know. So dat dragon gonna do what Thordane tells her. Don't kick over the spittoon, Urgo, if you know what I mean. We got it good here."

Satia grabbed Septimus's arm and whispered, "The draconian was telling the truth. They told Nox that they have you captive to make her do what Thordane tells her to do."

Septimus snarled, fingers digging into the dirt. "My mother is smart. If they don't let her see me, she won't believe them for long. Then they'll have a fight on their hands for sure."

"And *that*," said a vicious, raspy voice that made them both jump, "is why you two are coming wif me."

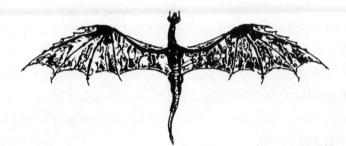

CHAPTER SIX

The hobgoblin stood nearly seven feet tall. He was broad at the shoulder, with biceps that looked bigger than wagon wheels. His hair was greenish and spiked up over his forehead. One brown eye bugged out at them while the other was covered by a thick leather patch. He shrugged a heavy iron club from his shoulder, pounding it into the wall so hard that the spikes made patterns in the thick wood. "OI! Urgo! Dugadee! Get out here, youse!"

The two hobgoblins inside slammed to their feet so fast that they overturned drinks, chairs, table, and all. Poking their heads out into the alley through the window, they stared at the larger hobgoblin with fear on their piggish faces. "Holg! I mean . . . yes, sir!" They scrambled through the window, shoving each other fiercely in their desperation to obey his command.

"Run!" Satia cried, tugging at Septimus's tunic.

"Oh, no you don't!" Holg slammed his massive

club against the barrel they'd hidden behind, knocking them over. The sheer force of the impact blew Satia's curly hair all around her face and she gasped as she fell to the muddy ground. Holg's hamlike fist grabbed the back of her shirt, lifting her easily, while Urgo and Dugadee grabbed Septimus despite the boy's wild thrashing. "These are the kids."

"You sure, boss?" Dugadee was the one with the high-pitched, wavery voice. As soon as he asked the question, he looked as though he regretted it, wincing and shivering back down to do his duty. He latched onto Septimus's arm and held on tightly. The ferocity that had served Septimus well against the draconians surfaced again, and the boy thrashed about wildly. But these hobgoblins were practiced in the fine art of dirty fighting, taking every punch and bite with flair and returning more than enough of their own. Fists flew, fangs sank into flesh, and within a few moments, the pile of arms and legs unraveled to reveal Dugadee sitting squarely on Septimus's back, with Urgo holding the boy's arms to the ground. "Rough one, boss!" Urgo winced, his eye already developing a black ring.

Holg's smile revealed more broken teeth than whole ones, and he lifted Satia up to stare her in the eye. He shoved his studded club into a leather hoop on his back and shook her hard enough to rattle her teeth. "Yeah. Dat's sure. We take 'em to the pits now, and then tell Thordane that they're under control. Might get a raise for this, boys!" When the two other hobgoblins perked up, Holg scowled lazily. "Me, I mean. Not you sods." Their faces fell.

Holg jerked Satia's short sword, the one she'd gotten from the fallen draconian, away from her. He stuffed it in his own belt with a grunt of covetousness. Satia kicked him, managing to dig her foot into his kneecap. She was rewarded with a shout, followed by a vicious growl. Limping, Holg grabbed a thin bit of rope from the horse stand at the front of the bar and twined it around her wrists, tying it tight before he tossed another to Urgo and Dugadee. They lashed Septimus's arms from wrist to elbow, sparing one of their belts to tie the boy's ankles as well.

Holg marched through the roughshod town, Satia trussed and tossed over his shoulder. Dugadee and Urgo followed behind, carrying the still-thrashing Septimus. All around them, hobgoblins looked up from their laughter, games of dice or arguing, watching as their leader carried the two children toward the castle as if they were festival hogs.

By the time they reached the gate of the crumbling castle, the sun had fully set. Instead of marching them through the gate to the keep, Holg took a narrow path along the lower wall into the quarry. His boots sank deep into the mud, squelching with every step, and the eyes that turned up toward them in the faint torchlight weren't brown or green, but wide and nearly colorless, shining up out of misshapen heads above scrawny necks. Half his size, the wretched-looking goblins hurled themselves out of Holg's path, but he went out of his way to kick them anyway, grumbling, "Slow gits! Get movin', get movin'! Night's no excuse not to finish yer work!"

Holg marched through a rusted gate and into the lower caverns of the keep. Clay-covered goblins, their greenish skin turned gray with crusted grime, slowly filled the big prison cells on either side. Near the end of the row, Holg paused and turned to grab the iron bars of one cell, chucking Satia in without a second thought. She slammed into a huge pile of mud and rolled messily to the filthy ground. Holg reached over, a sharp knife in his hand. With a quick jerk, he cut a tuft of Septimus's hair and jammed it into his pocket. "Put the boy in there too. Might as well use 'em as labor till Thordane decides what to do with 'em."

Urgo and Dugadee were only too happy to get rid of their burden, throwing Septimus in after Satia with great relish. The boy flew across the room, colliding with five of the goblins and toppling everyone down into the squishy, muddy floor.

"Get busy!" They slammed the door closed and Holg laughed. "That's done, then. I'll get talking to Thordane in the morning." He marched away with the merry saunter of a job well done, the other two burly hobgoblins puffing out their chests and following in his path. The last of the goblins trailed in behind them, and a little shadow slithered along the mud just before the rusted iron gate slammed shut. One by one, the hobgoblin guards walked the central corridor, shoving the last of their laborers into the cells and locking the cell doors behind them. The goblins reached through the bars to tug their trousers, but the hobgoblins glared at them. "No food till you've built the bricks!" spat one, smacking the hands away.

The goblins slunk back into their cells and reached into thick piles of mud lumped in the center of each floor—the same as the one that Satia landed on in their own cell. Only it wasn't just any mud, Satia saw. This was the thick kind, clay mud, the kind that could be sculpted and formed. In each cell it was the same: the goblins sat in circles around the mud piles, mashing the clay as if they were kneading bread, which Satia figured must be to get it to the right consistency. Then they packed it into rough wooden molds to dry into bricks, though Satia wasn't sure how the bricks would dry down here in this damp cell. Each of the goblins performed this work routinely, as if they'd done it a thousand times before. But in the cell where Satia and Septimus landed, the goblins didn't dare approach the mud pile for fear of their new cell mates.

"Holg didn't even bother to untie us." Satia squirmed, disgusted at the mud clinging to her side where she'd landed. She looked up at the scrawny, terrified little goblins that clustered at the other wall, staring at them. Those under Septimus squealed with horror, shoving him off as if the boy were on fire. They scrambled to either side, slipping in the muck as they fled. Satia caught a last glimpse of Holg and his men going out the rusted cellar gate and up the thin, raised path. "That beast took my sword, but he didn't find my knife. Septimus, can you roll over to me and get it out of my boot?"

"No." He struggled, lashing back and forth along the ground. "I'm stuck in this mud! You, goblin! Untie me!" he yelled, but the little goblins clustered even farther away, colorless eyes wide.

"Don't scare them even more!" Satia protested, using the slipperiness of the mud to sling herself around. She landed on her stomach, lifting her face out of the mud to glare at the wildly thrashing boy. "Septimus! They'll never let us go if they think we're dangerous! Look at them. These goblins are terrified. I don't even think they can understand our language. As much as I hate feeling pity for creatures like these, they're obviously not our enemies."

"Everyone is our enemy." Black hair fell across his eyes. Septimus snapped his teeth at the huddled mass, and the goblins shrieked.

"That's not true," Satia huffed, struggling against her bonds. "These goblins have been mistreated, and they're frightened. I've met goblins before, you know. I know a lot about them—"

"They have goblins in the palace at Gwynned?" Septimus snorted arrogantly.

Clearly, her original lie wasn't working anymore. Time to make up a new one. "Well, no, but when I said my father was a prince, I misspoke." Satia tossed her hair, thinking quickly. "What I meant to say is that he *works* with the prince. He's a wealthy merchant. He travels all over the place, you know, so he tells me a lot of things about the world. I know a lot more than you give me credit for."

There was a long pause, and his black eyes met hers in a measuring stare. Satia could feel sweat rising at her temples and along the back of her neck. Did the dragon have some way of magically telling that she was lying? Why did she keep *doing* this? If she hadn't lied to the cleric back in town, she'd still be in that safe inn room back in Gwynned.

"Well . . . you do seem pretty smart. And you did know where to hide when we were in that alley . . ." Septimus lingered on the problem, trying to force it to make sense.

Jumping in quickly before he could see the flaws in her logic, Satia snapped, "Listen to me, Septimus. These goblins—we're *not* going to hurt them."

A deep, strangely sonorous voice cut in on their argument, making Satia jump half out of her skin. "Do you mean that?" She jerked her head around as best she could in her bonds, struggling to make out the speaker. Her eyes focused on movement in the back corner of the cell, behind the mass of goblins. The voice spoke in unaccented Common, and the goblins parted with a sigh, as if they'd hoped to hear it. Beyond the goblins sat a larger figure with his back pressed against the wall. He might have been wearing a tunic and trousers, but Satia honestly couldn't tell through all the crusted mud. A thick gray beard hung halfway down his chest, and the color of his skin was pale—or at least she guessed it was. He was definitely human, male, and adult, but his blue eyes were the only thing about him that had any color at all.

"Of course I mean that." Satia rolled over on her side, unable to hold her head up anymore. It fell sideways into the mud, which squished against her ear. "Ew."

The man slowly untangled himself from the huddled goblins, pushing their arms and legs away from him. Satia wasn't sure if the goblins had been trying to hide and protect him, or if they'd been trying to tug him out of his little muddy divot in the corner. Who could tell with goblins?

The man walked as if he hadn't moved in weeks, limping gingerly on withered limbs and leaning on the goblins that surrounded him like a skirt. "Yet you have a knife in your boot. If you get free, you could use it."

"On the hobgoblins, not on you." Satia stole a moment to glare witheringly at Septimus before he could chime in, seeing the boy snap his mouth shut with a grumpy hiss. "We just want to get out of here."

With a sigh, the man answered, "We all do." He knelt down beside her and started fumbling in the leg of Satia's boot. "But even if you could get out of this cell, fight the hobgoblins guarding the prison, and then sneak across the quarry, the draconians up there are watching for anyone leaving the keep. They'd catch you before you got ten paces down the road, and you'd never make the forest. Ah. Here it is." He pulled out her little dagger, turning it over in his hand. The goblins whimpered, several scattering to the far side of the mud pile and peering out curiously from all sides.

"If I let you go," the old man said, eyes falling again to meet Satia's, "do you promise not to harm any of the goblins here? Your word of honor?" He glanced over to Septimus, and Satia wished she was close enough to kick her traveling companion.

"I promise," she said. "And he promises too."

Septimus gave his bonds one last tug, desperately trying to break them. At last, seeing no other way out, he slumped down into the mud and let his arms and legs fall still. "Fine. I promise," he muttered through his teeth.

"Good." The old man's hands shook slightly as he approached the ropes, and he paused to still himself. Then he slashed through the ties on Satia's arms. She sat up quickly, rubbing the mud out of her face.

The goblins jumped back, whispering among themselves. "Go ahead, friends," the man told them kindly. "Get to work so we can all be fed." Reassured, they plunged their hands into the mud pile to start making bricks as fast as their little spindly arms would allow.

Satia pushed herself to her feet, watching the

old man haltingly walk toward Septimus. He paused along the way, as though the journey wearied him, then lowered himself to his knees beside the boy and began working on the ropes with Satia's knife. "Who are you?" she asked.

"My name," he said wearily, "is Mosango." The ropes around Septimus's wrists broke apart under Satia's knife, and Septimus cried out sharply. Mosango jerked back his hand, but there was a faint trace of red on Septimus's forearm. "My apologies, lad," Mosango said tiredly. "I am an old man, and my eyes are not so good." Indeed, he fumbled a bit trying to find Septimus's ankles so that he could cut the belt.

Septimus snatched the knife away from Mosango. "I'll do it," he growled, scooting away. "I'd rather you not cut off my feet."

The goblins struggled over the pile, their little arms sunk up to the elbows in mud. They piled filled brick molds more swiftly than Satia could imagine, packing them with bits of straw to keep the mud from sticking to the molds. "Who are you and what are you doing here?" Satia asked.

His wrinkled face creaked into a smile, and she realized he was about to ask the same question. He did her the courtesy of answering first, bowing to her in an archaic, courtly fashion as he rose to his feet. "Some years ago I did Lord Thordane the dishonor of visiting his city and drinking too much of his ale. There was a tussle, some words were exchanged, and I struck out at his hobgoblin commander, Holg. He returned the favor by placing me here." He shrugged, his beard waggling against his chest. "And you?"

"We're trying to find Septimus's mother," Satia answered. "Thordane kidnapped her." A scowl from the boy was enough to make her forget the rest of her sentence—the part about both Septimus and his mother being dragons. She was willing to lie about her own background. Might as well extend the favor to her new "friend."

Mosango nodded soberly. "A brave quest indeed. Sadly, one that seems finished." He walked across the room gingerly and lowered himself once more against the wall. One of the goblins reached out and patted Mosango's boot, leaving a muddy palm print on the old man's already grimy boot. "You're here, like me, and you'll be here for the rest of your life." He sighed. "Also like me." A shadow moved across the bars out in the hallway, and Septimus hissed at them to lower their voices, scooting away from the bars. They fell silent for a moment, letting only the crackle of the hobgoblin torches in the hall and the slick, wet sound of brick making fill the cell.

Finally Satia got up the courage to continue the conversation. "What do you mean?" She crawled over to sit at the man's feet so they could talk without drawing the guards' attention. Septimus moved closer as well, apparently less disturbed by the mud than Satia was. She tried to scrape some of the filth off her trousers, muttering, "There's a way in, so there's got to be a way out."

"These goblins"—Mosango waved his hand gently to encompass the hardworking laborers—"have been here for six years. I've been in the pits even longer. The only time Thordane comes down here is when he's looking for something to use as bait on one of his dragon hunts. These goblins are the Howlback tribe. They were captured stealing cows from the hobgoblin encampment during a particularly harsh winter. Now they have to pay back the cows they stole, in steel. They get paid for working here . . . but they also get all of their food and shelter taken out of their pay."

"So how much do they end up making?" Septimus asked suspiciously.

"Nothing." Mosango shook his head. "Nothing at all."

Satia choked. "That's horrible!"

"That's the way Lord Thordane operates. There's

nothing that can be done, you see. Once you come down to the prisons, you're here forever."

"It's not true. You've just given up hope!" Satia got up and scrambled to the bars. They were wide apart enough that she could stick her head through and peer up and down the hallway. She saw several hobgoblins standing by the quarry door, though none of them looked back at her. Jerking back, she spun to face Septimus and Mosango. "Those hobgoblins are bored out of their minds. They won't even notice if we sneak out of here."

"But the bars—" Septimus started.

Satia cut him off. "I can get through a rusty lock." Septimus and Mosango both stared at her, and Satia felt her face heat up like one of the hobgoblin torches. "I . . . uh . . . my father . . . I mean . . ." Her voice faltered. Septimus crossed his arms and harrumphed. "Shut up. I can get us out. That's all you need to know." She sat down and crossed her arms, fuming. For once in their short time together, Septimus didn't ask the obvious question. She wasn't sure if that made her feel better . . . or worse.

With a strange, frightened look on his face, Mosango raised his arms and waved his hands back and forth in warning. "No, no, no! You can't! You'll get us all in trouble. Even if you succeed, it will only be more difficult for our little friends. I can't allow them to come to harm. They've been kind to me."

"They're goblins!" Satia and Septimus burst out together.

Mosango's eyes narrowed, the color vanishing among his deep wrinkles. "They are my friends, and they are decent folk, for goblins. My hands, they shake," he held them out so the children could see. "I cannot make bricks, and I am too old to dig in the mud all day. The goblins do my share of the work, and in exchange I tell them stories of my days in Solamnia—tales of knights and of bravery, things that cheer them in their work."

"Solamnia! Then . . . you're a knight?" Satia asked.

"Well, yes," Mosango said, confused by the question. "Of course."

The goblin that had touched Mosango's leg spoke, startling Satia. "Mosango, friend." His green skin shone in the torchlight, greasy with water and mud. It took him a moment to gather his courage and mutter more. "No hurt Mosango."

"You see?" beamed the old knight. "Very good friends. I can't let you hurt them by trying to escape."

Satia sat back, trying to think of a way out. She could tell that if she didn't come up with an idea soon,

Septimus was going to try to escape anyway—goblins or no goblins. "We can't escape, and we can't stay here. Only one choice, then." Both of them stared at her curiously, and the goblin turned, unconcerned, to sniff at the shadows in the corridor.

"One of us is going to have to die."

CHAPTER SEVEN

That morning was the least pleasant dawn that Satia could remember. In the past, she'd woken up in the sewers of Gwynned, in back alleyways filled with trash, even on rocks down by the wharf—and this, she had to say, was worse. She fell asleep sitting up last night because lying down in the mud was suicide, and her head had been thrust into the corner of the wall for support. Now, her neck ached from the position, her hair was thick and clumped with mud where it had stuck to the wall, and a goblin— probably trying to be helpful—had half buried her in a thick, nasty blanket made of horsehair. All in all, disgusting.

The horrible ringing sound in her ear wasn't from the position in which she slept, but was instead caused by a hobgoblin marching up and down the corridor and clanging a rusted sword against the bars, ringing a withering wake-up call. Already the goblins were climbing over one another to get to the scraps that had been tossed on iron trays in front of the bars. The trays did little to keep the scraps out of the mud, but by the smell of the food, a little dirt would probably make it taste better.

"Ugh." Satia stretched, trying to get her senses in order and rub out the aches in her muscles. Septimus snatched scraps away from goblins and scarfed them down. Mosango did the same, but with far more courtesy to his little green friends. "Guess I'm the only one who's not hungry."

The prisoners were whipped out into the hall by another hobgoblin, who didn't bother replacing their bonds. Several goblins from each cell were assigned to carrying out the previous night's brick molds—probably to dry in the sun somewhere they wouldn't get wet.

Satia could see that what Mosango said yesterday was true: even if they ran, the hobgoblins on the walls of the quarry would shoot them down with crossbows. The heavy mud sides of the quarry prevented any real climbing, even if the hobgoblins were distracted, and the only opening into the keep was the gated passageway to the dungeon where the goblins were kept. Satia sighed, falling into line with the rest. This was going to be hard.

There was a pile of wicker baskets, each one nearly as big as a goblin, in a little shack outside the dungeon door. Everybody took one, and a hobgoblin shoved the handle of a basket into Satia's hand along with the rest. Some of the goblins made a second stop, loading small balsa-wood boxes gingerly into their baskets. One of them gulped as he lifted the basket to his shoulder as smoothly as possible.

"Demolitions," Mosango whispered to Septimus. "They're carrying the explosives that they'll use to blow down the next part of the quarry wall. The ammunition is made of oil and other stuff I'm not sure of. Thordane makes them himself, just for us."

"Lucky goblins." Sarcasm dripped from the words. Septimus flicked long fingernails against his own wicker basket. "I bet they're being punished by the others for eating too much or not working fast enough, eh?"

"On the contrary," Mosango retorted in a stern, colorless tone. "They're the bravest of us all."

Indeed, the six goblins with balsa boxes walked to the front of the line with even, halting steps, and the other goblins parted silently before them. It was like watching a military parade—except covered in grime—for all the respect and honor that Satia could see in the other goblins' faces. They moved to the front of the line, and the other workers started up a low, sad-sounding chant in a language Satia didn't know. Only when the six were several steps ahead did the main body of workers begin to move.

The clay pit was a massive area, larger than the keep above it, and stretched out over a good half mile. The bottom of it was several stories below them, thick and wet with the remnants of a stream that once flowed into the swamp. Now all it did was thicken the mud at the bottom of the pit into a thigh-deep sludge, so deep that the goblins ordered to go to the bottom had to carry their wicker baskets on their heads. Paths skitter-scattered up and down all sides of the quarry, with wide ledges where mud had fallen, leaving the occasional shelf of stone. The hobgoblins were generous with their whips, urging the goblins to their posts. The six went to the side of quarry just to the east of the keep and started placing the balsa-wood boxes in cracks along the muddy wall.

"You're sure about this?" Mosango whispered to Satia warily. "Once this plan gets started, we won't be able to stop it. It will go downhill as fast as . . . well, as fast as that mud slides. My lady, you are most courageous to attempt this, but I want to be certain that you still intend to go through with it."

"It's the only way. If they think Septimus and I

are dead, then they won't hurt the goblins for helping us escape. Just keep your eyes open in case anything goes wrong. And . . . thanks, Mosango." Satia reached out and squeezed the limping old man's hand. "If we get out of here, we'll see what we can do to help you someday too."

He smiled with an odd cheerfulness. "Paladine be with you, little one."

Instead of making her feel better, his words felt heavy on Satia's shoulders. Paladine? She glanced over at Septimus, who was scowling as usual. Well, who knows. Paladine was a generous god. He might understand why she was working with a black dragon to free another black dragon . . . or maybe she could just explain it to him when she died and went to see him. Paladine was a god. He seemed reasonable. Maybe if she gave it just a little tweak of the facts he'd be on her side—right?

"Hope you're not having second thoughts," Septimus hissed as he moved closer. "We only get one chance at this."

Satia shoved him, not caring if she jabbed his ribs. "I know what to do. It's my plan, isn't it?"

"Yeah, but it's the only plan we've got." His sharp-toothed grin took a little of the sting out of his words. There was no time to reply, for one of the big hobgoblins stepped up behind them and cuffed them both across the back of their shoulders, shoving them closer to the front of the line. Satia obeyed, catching up with the goblins at the head of the main group, just a few paces behind those with the balsa-wood boxes.

"Holg wants you two near the front," grumped the hobgoblin, clearly still sleepy. "So you stay up there!" He kept his voice low, a mere rumble, rather than the bullying shout he'd used the night before.

"Works for me," Septimus said, trying to hide his customary wicked grin. "Closer to the detonations, closer to freedom." Satia nodded sharply in agreement once, hoping that the hobgoblin guards were all as bleary as that one.

When they reached the mud slope, Mosango pointed with one slim finger toward an area of the wall. Satia wouldn't have noticed it at first, but she could tell that the goblins around her were well aware of the deficiency in the muddy slope. There was a stone ledge, U-shaped and slightly open behind the mud. It was a narrow aperture, but solid—it would protect them from the blast. Now, to get close enough to it that the hobgoblins wouldn't notice when they slipped inside . . .

The hobgoblins cracked their whips above the goblins in the front, and the small creatures scuttled forward with fear in every wide, glassy eye. They crawled gingerly up and down the slope of the muddy hill, finding nooks and crevices in which to place their little boxes. "How do the boxes work?" Satia tugged on Mosango's torn and muddy sleeve.

"They're very delicate. One loud noise and *blam!* They go off. I'm not sure what they're made of, but they aren't magic, as far as I can tell."

"Loud noise?" asked Septimus. "Is that why all the guards are whispering?"

"Well, yes, that and the hangovers," Mosango winked in reply.

The goblins crawled down the slope one by one after they'd placed their boxes, whimpering with the effort it took to keep still and move quietly. The first one to the bottom rushed back to the others, who embraced him with their wizened, muddy arms. Yet more of the goblins wrung their hands, choking back nervous whispers as they watched the other members of their tribe wriggling down the filthy hillside.

One of the box carriers jerked to a halt, tugging at his ankle. Satia could see vines twisted around the goblin's foot, holding him fast. "Mosango, how do they set off the boxes?"

"There's a gong up there," the old man turned

and pointed into the glare of the rising sun. "The hobgoblins will strike it precisely at full sunrise. That's what triggers the detonation. Should go off any minute now."

"Can they see that he's up there?"

"What?" Mosango twisted to look at her. "Who?"

"The goblin! Can they tell that he's stuck?" Frantic now, Satia started climbing up the hill. Septimus grabbed her and jerked her back. "You can't go up there! If you do, you'll both die, and that won't help me get free."

"Charming. But I'm going." Satia smacked away Septimus's hands and raced up the mud slope on hands and knees, gripping any root or lump of stone that would bear her weight. Below, the goblins clustered around even as the hobgoblins got out their whips to drive them back from the edge of the slope.

Satia heard Septimus turn on them, all snarls and gnashing teeth. "Get back, you little fools, or you'll all die!" He might not have his dragonfear right now, since his magic was bound by his mother's spell, but the goblins seemed absolutely terrified of the ball of wrath in their midst. They ran from Septimus with even more horror than from the whips. A little bit of pandemonium broke out below as the hobgoblins tried to figure out what was going on. Goblins clustered around Mosango, alternately hiding behind him and preparing to ineptly defend him. Septimus raged in silence, smacking the goblins ever farther from the slope.

Well, they'd hoped for a distraction, but the nook seemed very far away, and the sun was almost over the horizon. Sliding through mud and tripping over vines, Satia reached the goblin at last, drawing her steel knife from her boot to saw away the entangling vines. The little green fellow gripped her shoulders in gratitude, babbling something in Goblin. "Yeah, you're welcome," she guessed, and grabbed his hand to swing him down the slope. The goblin's scrawny fingers locked onto hers, his ratty clothing flapping around his legs as he launched himself out toward the others.

Just then, the sun crested the horizon, blinding them both with a brilliant ray of light. In that frozen, gleaming moment, Satia heard a low ringing at the edge of her consciousness. In an instant, the ringing became a note, the note became thunderous, and then the ground shook under her feet as the little balsa-wood boxes exploded at the sound of the gong. The goblin's fingers slipped from her grasp. The sunlight was so bright in her face that she wasn't sure which direction the nook was, where to hide—and it was all but too late.

Even as she hurled herself from the slope, desperately hoping she remembered where the ledge was, the entire slope erupted into stone and mud. If she could just reach that little nook, it would shelter her from the blast, hiding her from the hobgoblins and enabling her to escape. But she'd wasted precious time rescuing the stuck goblin. The nook seemed very far away, more than fifteen feet to the left and down the rocky slope. She'd have to jump for it.

Earth exploded all around Satia, thick mud flying in every direction. Stones pelted her arms and legs as she balled up under the deluge. There was a sound much like a tearing noise—of stone sliding away from earth—and the entire side of the hill began to tremble and collapse. Satia, half blinded by the sun and deafened by the sound of explosion after explosion going off all around her, dived for the nook.

Satia could hear Septimus yelling, see the larger figure of Mosango surrounded by shrieking goblins. She scrabbled along the muddy face of the hill, fingers clawing and wrapping around the edge of the crevice that would shelter her—and then the mud slide hit. Rocks, mud, and thousands of pounds of earth slammed into her side, sending Satia spinning from the lip of the avalanche. She was pounded downward, feet over head amid the massive weight of the mud.

The last thing Satia saw was a dark flow of earth that bore her over the edge of the crevice. It was followed by a terrible, crushing weight.

Then, there was nothing at all.

CHAPTER EIGHT

G et back!" roared Septimus, spreading his fingers wide and arching his back. He leaped between the scurrying goblins and the collapsing quarry wall, batting at one little fellow with enough force to knock the goblin back toward the group. Septimus bared his teeth and stomped forward, watching as the goblins shrieked and fled the other way. That was good. The mud slide behind them had swept over Satia before she could even scream, and it kept coming with a giant rumble.

Mosango—that stringy old waste—was trying to gather the goblins together like some sort of herd beast. What did he know about making prey clump? Septimus had learned such lessons at the wing of his mother, driving flocks of sheep to the slaughter. He knew exactly what to do.

Leaping in front of one of the loudest goblins, Septimus slapped him right in the face, leaving red marks across his green face. The goblin responded as Septimus hoped, shrieking loudly enough to make the others start up in empathy, and soon the whole group was turning to flee. The hobgoblins behind them started snapping their black whips, cracking them down on the goblins to try and maintain order.

Too late for that. Furious and driven by the pandemonium all around him, Septimus charged through the center of the goblins and lunged ferally at one of the big guards. The hobgoblin screamed in surprise and flailed about with his whip as Septimus knocked him over. Two more hobgoblins dived in on the boy, punching and kicking him. Septimus didn't care. Satia was dead.

One of the hobgoblins delivered a punch to the side of Septimus's head that sent the whole world spinning, and he could swear that he could still hear the rumble of the avalanche rolling in his ears. Septimus felt a swoop of air, and then the ground was bouncing beneath him, wind swishing all about him as if he were moving—but he couldn't lift either arms or legs. Cold, hard stone slammed against his back and scraped up his side, and then he spun to a nauseating stop. Wobbling his head off the ground, Septimus stared up at the black boots of one of the hobgoblin guards and tried to hiss in defiance.

Mosango's old, wrinkled hands finally pulled him off, even as the hobgoblins laughed and kicked Septimus again. Septimus growled, snapping feebly at the old man's hands. Everything was spinning. It was like the wonderful vertigo of flying, but a lot more bruised. He looked up into the sky and saw two small red dragons wheeling among the clouds, looking down at all the fuss happening within the quarry. Vex and Beset, no doubt, enjoying the panic below. For a horrible moment, Septimus wondered if he'd ever be up there again. He looked away quickly, and tried not to look back again.

"He'll be all right." Mosango's voice sounded distant, though the old man's face was right up in his, breathing that stinky cow breath right into Septimus's muzzle. Nose, he thought blearily. I have a nose now. "He just took a nasty crack from Dugadee's big bronze-knuckled glove, that's all." The goblins cooed in terror, huddling around them. "Can you hear me, Septimus?" Mosango asked. "Can you say anything?"

"I want to kill them," Septimus managed, licking his teeth to be sure they were all still in place.

Mosango smiled. "He's fine. Spunky little fellow too."

Holg's voice was next to come into focus, yelling and whipping his own hobgoblins. ". . . worth more than the lot of you! I'll break hide the next time that one takes such a shot! You hear me, you low-life, rotgut filth?"

Holg stood over him then, jerking Septimus up by the chest of his shirt. "He still alive?" Holg asked Mosango, staring down Septimus's throat and into his eyes.

"He needs to rest. I'll take him back to the cell and make sure he turns out fine." Mosango tugged on Septimus, cautiously encouraging Holg to lower the boy to his feet. "There's too much work to do to make one of the goblins do it. I can handle it just fine."

Holg scoured Mosango with a nervous, angry stare. Perhaps he realized that Mosango was right—or perhaps he was thinking more about the bottom line of mud digging than about the old man's health. But whatever his motivation, the hobgoblin let them go. "Do it. But if'n I find you runnin' away wif him, I'll pound you both into bricks."

Mosango didn't dignify Holg's threat with an answer. He wrapped Septimus's arm about his shoulders—though the old man could barely stand on his own feet—and started the trek back toward the dungeons while the goblins dug fiercely into the clay.

"No!" Septimus tried to fight against the old man's

suddenly steely fingers. "Satia. We have to help her. She's under there. She promised me . . . my mother . . ."

"Septimus, calm down."

"Satia can't be dead. If she's dead I'll never free my mother. So she can't be dead, right?" He fought to contain his instincts and apply reason. This could be worked out. There had to be a way. "We start there."

Mosango blinked, trying to follow the rush of words. "Are you all right?"

"Satia's a liar. She lies all the time. Satia being dead—that's just another of her lies. She's lying about being dead, just like she kept lying about her father in Gwynned. It's not true. This is her plan, right? The hobgoblins were supposed to think she was dead. It's working. It's just working too well. But that's all right— we just have to believe in it." Septimus stomped his foot, wishing he could sweep his wings out majestically in punctuation like his mother did when she was serious about something. "I can plan for this. I can make this work, just like I made things work when they got complicated in Gwynned. I just need a little time, a plan—"

"Well, I can't fault your logic." Mosango quirked his eyebrow and continued in a whisper, "And if she can be dug out, I swear to you, the Howlback tribe will find her. They're the most excellent diggers—and they've got a reason. Satia saved the life of one of their tribe. They owe her."

"They'll find her?"

"They will, if anyone can. But they'll do it quietly so the hobgoblins won't notice. Now come on, before Holg thinks too clearly about letting you go into the dungeons instead of staying where he can keep an eye on you." Mosango dragged Septimus along, for the boy's pride wouldn't let him be carried. The goblins shot worried looks at them from across the quarry while their hands scrabbled roughly at the clay.

"Satia's smart. She's got the knowledge of your kind, you humans. Half the time we think you're dead, you just come right back again." Septimus spat the words, not sounding worried, angry that she dared die and leave him right in the middle of everything. "We made a deal, she and I," he snarled.

"I'm sure she'll keep to it. Word of honor, you know." Mosango looked back over his shoulder as he reached to open the dungeon door. Septimus followed his glance and saw that the goblins had already dug several deep holes throughout the muddy avalanche . . . but they had come up with nothing more than rocks and stones.

"How long can you humans breathe under rocks?" Septimus asked.

"Not long," Mosango answered softly.

"Probably less, the way Satia spends all her air talking all the time," the boy mused.

Mosango cleared his throat, his blue eyes troubled. "Why do you keep calling us 'you humans' and 'your kind'? Aren't you human too, son?"

Septimus eyed him, pushing away and stomping weakly into their cell. "Not for much longer, if I can help it. I was born a dragon, and I intend to go back to being one as soon as they dig up Satia, stick her back on her funny two-legged feet, and we can get back to the plan." All of the anger and the strange, tingly emotion that had come upon him when Satia disappeared beneath the flood of stone came out in a roar: "I have to save my mother!"

He expected the old man to laugh at him, to disbelieve his statement. Septimus spread his legs, hands on his hips, and flared his nostrils in what he hoped was as intimidating a manner as possible, but Mosango wasn't paying attention. The old man slid down the wall to his usual seat and tugged on his beard. "Dragon, eh?" he considered. "I used to know one of those."

Choking on his tongue, Septimus managed to ask, "Who?"

"Coppery-colored fellow. Named . . . what was it?" Mosango squinched his eyes half shut, trying to remember. "Pot. Kettle. No, that's not it. Glick! No . . . Gleamfire. Yes, that was it."

"Never knew him," Septimus grumped, but there was a gleam in Mosango's eye that hadn't been there before. "But then again, I'm very young. I don't know many dragons besides my mother."

"Flew with him during the war. War of the Lance, you know, against Takhisis and her crew. When I was a Knight of Solamnia. We rode into the sunrise, the shine of metal wings like a sword on the horizon. I remember holding the lance, I remember the horns . . ." Suddenly, Mosango jerked out of his reverie and sat up straight, as if something had jabbed him. "I'll help you, son."

"What?"

"Even if they don't find Satia—that poor, sweet, brave girl—I'll help you. I still remember my oath to Paladine and his dragons, the feel of the wind under me, the lance in my hand. I'll help you in the name of my old companions. It will be like riding the winds again when I was a knight, when the glory of battle was enough to remind me that things could go right in the world."

"What are you babbling about?" Septimus blinked, stunned, as the knight leaped to his scrawny feet and pumped his fist in the air.

"For Solamnia! For Paladine!" Mosango stared down at Septimus, his blue eyes shining with the light of renewed fervor. "For your mother!" Something had snapped inside the old man's memory, an old vigor. He stood upright, weaving a little and looking very much like a stalk of celery, all wiry body and crazy tufted hair. "For the Lady Satia's honor, and for her memory." He placed his hand with sudden solemnity on Septimus's shoulder. "Although, of course, she's not dead."

Septimus could only nod, stunned.

"We'll free your mother, my boy, I promise you. It'll be just like the old days in Paladine's service."

Septimus opened his mouth. To his credit, he really thought about correcting the old man, telling him that his mother wasn't one of Paladine's metallic dragons, but instead a black-scaled dragon born in Takhisis's service. Yes, Nox hadn't been part of the war, but still . . . Staring up at Mosango's blazing eyes, Septimus could tell the old man wouldn't understand the fine delicacies of dragon politics. Chromatic dragons: evil. Metallic dragons: good. That was all the Solamnic Knights ever cared about.

"That's great, Mosango," Septimus nodded, shoving the black hair out of his eyes. "My mother will be so . . ."—he searched for a good word—"er . . . happy?"

"Boy!" roared a voice at the end of the hallway.

"The Ogre King gonna see you now!" Holg and two of his goons marched into the dungeon, clubs at their sides.

"Ogre King?" Septimus whispered.

"He's Thordane's right-hand man—in charge of the quarry," Mosango answered, under his breath. He stood up straighter and took Septimus's hand. "The boy's injured, Holg. He was hurt in the rock collapse. I'm going to have to go with him to make sure he can stand up in front of the Ogre King."

"Fine by me." Holg reached in with one ham hand and grabbed Mosango's arm, jerking them both out of the cell. "Don't matter to me if'n you go, stay, or die, old man. Never much use for you anyway, not since you sold your armor for booze in the town." Holg's smile was evil, all teeth and glinting eye. "Drink didn't help you forget the boy you kill't, did it, Mosango?"

All the strength and joy abruptly drained out of the old man's face, leaving him as shattered and weak as before. He half withered in Holg's grasp, deflating like a balloon.

"Mosango, what does he mean?" Septimus wriggled as the other hobgoblins grabbed him. "Mosango?" But the man lay in Holg's grasp, not fighting, not struggling at all as the hobgoblins tied their arms and kicked them down the corridor toward the meeting with their master. Septimus hardly noticed the rough hands or the cord around his wrists. What boy? What was Holg talking about?

What had Mosango done?

CHAPTER NINE

Something with shining eyes devoid of color jerked her from her warm cocoon into cold air and darkness. Hands tugged at her, and then the wind slammed into her lungs with all the power of a siege engine. Satia gasped and scrabbled at her burning throat. The cough shook her, waking her numb mind. How long had she been under there? And who was this ragged lump patting her on the back?

She sat in the darkness, trying to control the racking coughs that shook her frame. She was in a cave or a tunnel of some kind, with only a thin trace of light illuminating the darkness. Now that she was breathing more normally, she could see her rescuer huddled over her like some kind of ragamuffin mother hen. It was a goblin dressed in green and brown scraps of fabric twisted tightly about the arms, legs and torso, and covered by a thick chest-armor piece of metal with flaps hanging down to either side of his hunched thighs. He had a long, crooked staff tied to his back, with a loop of cord, vials, feathers, and other primitive-looking trinkets dangling from an oddly tilted crossbar strapped to the rag-wrapped staff. It was utilitarian, just like the pouches hanging from his belt and the twin daggers strapped to his forearms.

"Get up, get up. No time to sit." The goblin tugged at her.

Scrambling to her knees, Satia looked behind her at the narrow crevice in the wall. She'd made it to the opening, but the avalanche on the far side looked much thicker than she'd thought it would be. "The last box," she realized. "It was in the wrong place. The goblin didn't make it up the hill." Cold chills ran down her spine as she realized it. "If that crevice hadn't led to this cave . . ."

"Yes, yes, get up. Lucky I was watching. Lucky I was here. Now stop whining and let's get going. Come on, human, get tough. Lots to do before we rest." The goblin blinked first one flat, liquid eye, then the other, his filthy smile taking the sting out of his words. He clucked all about her, helping her to her feet, warning her about the low ceiling, even reminding her to take her knife out of her boot and hold it in her hand.

Exasperated, Satia burst out, "Who are you?"

"Gneech."

Not sure if the odd little goblin had given her his name or if it was a sneeze, Satia stammered, "Grinch?"

"Gneech," he repeated, patting her knee. "Druid of the Howlback. Like priest, but priest for goblin. Herbs, plants, fire, and smoke. Come on, now."

"Druid of the Howlback? The tribe in the quarry? But I didn't see you down there."

"No, nor will. I'm free. Trying to pay their price, get them out." His flat face fell. "Or not, and stay here forever. Hoping that won't be the case. I said come now. Time to go." Clearly, Gneech wasn't used to being contradicted.

They trudged through tiny back caverns, some as narrow as Satia was wide. Gneech slipped through them easily—he was apparently made of stretchy tree sap—while she had to tug and shove her way through. More mud dripped down the walls, leaking and dripping down over them in thick, slimy coils. For all Satia could tell, they were marching in a circle through the quarry wall, covering the same disgusting territory. Only the constant sound of running water, always to their left, gave her any sign that they were making headway.

"Where are we going?"

"To save your friends." Gneech laughed back over his shoulder, pausing to dig something up from the mud at his feet. From the sound of squeaking, it was a rat. From the sudden crunch, it was dinner.

"My friends aren't in danger. They were nowhere near the avalanche." She tried not to look at his mouth, blessing the dimness for once.

"Not the avalanche. The Ogre King wants to see them. I hear Holg shouting about it in the keep. Come, this back way to the keep. But now we have to get through river."

Satia paused. She'd gotten away from Septimus. Why would she want to get into any more trouble? Noticing her hesitance, Gneech turned a narrow eye on her, the ridge of his eyebrow quirking sagely. "You do want to save friends, yes?"

Did she? Septimus kidnapped her. He dragged her out here, got her attacked by a wizard, trudged through a marsh, and wanted her to free an evil black dragon and let her loose on the world. But then again, neither Nox nor Septimus had been involved in the War of the Lance. And if she didn't get him out, how was she going to get home? A hundred different scenarios flashed through her head, none of them good. But most of all, she'd made a promise, and she didn't intend for that promise to turn out to be a lie.

"Yes," she answered Gneech. "I want to save my friends."

The goblin druid nodded sagely and trundled forward into the muck.

Satia didn't have to ask what he meant by "river"—it was apparent all too quickly. From the smell of it, it hadn't been a real river in a very long time. Choked with sewage and filth from the fortress above, the slightly stirring channel of water coughed up bubbles of sulfurous waste. She'd thought the *mud* was bad.

"We have to swim in that?" Covering her nose didn't help much. Covering her whole head probably wouldn't help much, either, considering how rank the smell was.

"Swim, run, fight. Sleep, if we need to. Anything to keep away from the hobgoblins." Gneech patted her shoulder. "It not so bad. You get used to it. Going to have to, if you want to help your friends." He waded out into the water, sinking up to his armpits in just a couple of steps. "You come now."

Satia stared at the lapping waves, revolted, trying not to question what the thicker chunks were. She raised a foot, then paused and set it down again. Adventure was supposed to be about shining armor, battlefields, and wizards with sparkling magic. Even in Gwynned, where the shadows were thick, adventure was about outsmarting your opponent, using the thieves' highway to vanish into the darkness.

Adventure was not—definitely not—about *filth*. "I don't—I mean, I've done this kind of thing before, of course. My father . . . in Gwynned . . ." The old lie suddenly didn't come easily to her lips, and she stared down at the rippling, thick waters. She opened her mouth to fabricate something else, but it fell apart before she could say anything at all.

Gneech ignored her. "Come on. What more important to you, girl—pride or the lives of your friends?" His weird, glittery eyes shone in the dim light, and his spindly fingers made ripples in the chunky syrup surrounding him. "Follow me." He was right. She gulped, and followed him.

The water clumped around Satia's legs and arms, thickly holding her up when she kicked off from the bank. Something long and snakelike twisted around her ankle, and she kicked it away, smothering a squeal. Gneech pretended not to notice. "This way." He swam to the wall, feeling along it until he found the opening. "You hold breath. Grab my feet. I pull you through."

"What's on the other side?"

"Hallway to the Ogre King's throne room. Dragons there. And soon, your friends and their guards."

"The hobgoblins won't find us?"

"No. Hobgoblins don't come this way. It too dirty for them."

"The dragons won't smell us?" she asked nervously.

Gneech snorted rudely. "Vex and Beset. Two little dragons about as smart as my stick." He gestured at the staff for emphasis. "Came out of eggs all alone, mother killed in great war. Thordane find them. Raise them. But they too small to ride, not old enough, so he has to capture big dragon. Still, they raised by human, not dragon—they don't know much about smelling things or hunting things. Only know what Thordane teach them, and that's not much beyond how to kill." Gneech shook his head. "Two stupid dragons. Now, into water with you!"

Satia groaned, but there was no time to protest, for Gneech bobbed under the water like a sinking stone. She grabbed his ankles and felt a hefty pull—this little fellow could swim like a fish! Holding her breath in a quick gulp, she squinched her eyes shut and followed along. All she could do was kick—and hope that the passage was short enough. The walls were tight around her, occasionally bumping against her legs as she kicked, and sometimes thick clumps of . . . something . . . would push past her in the narrow hole. They went downward first, causing Satia an almost uncontrollable surge of panic, but then cut back up again, apparently traveling via narrow sewage routes beneath the keep.

Maybe Gneech didn't need to breathe. Maybe he could keep his eyes open in this sludge without them burning out of his head. Whatever it was that allowed him to find this disgusting path, Satia blessed it—and prayed to various unnamed gods that he'd find the surface soon!

They broke through at last, and Satia took in a deep breath of air, half choking on the stench. She tried to wipe some of the syrupy water out of her eyes, opening them cautiously. They were in a small room made of carved stone—not a cavern—where the small pool of water from which they climbed seemed to be tucked away from prying eyes. She could see a hallway through the arched opening and hear quiet noises off somewhere else in the keep. Gneech pointed at a trickle of running water above them that coiled down the wall. He reached out to splash some of it onto his bald head and over his possessions, wiping off some of the worst of the muddy black gunk that clung to him.

Satia reached to do the same, but a sudden noise in the hallway startled her. "Keep moving!" yelled a guard. "Not far now, and then you can fall down dead all you want!" Barking laughter followed the insult. Satia recognized those voices—Urgo and Dugadee.

"No time!" Gneech slapped her hands away from

the water and jerked the lopsided staff from his back. "They here!" He charged into the hallway, his slapping feet leaving watery footprints on the stone. Satia groaned, glanced longingly at the clean trickle, and then ran after him.

Indeed, Dugadee and Urgo stood in the hallway, shoving a bound Mosango before them. Septimus had his hands tied as well, but he was looped at the end of a four-foot pole. Satia supposed it was to keep the boy from kicking Urgo in the shins. Based on the way the hobgoblin was already limping, the pole was a recent addition to Septimus's bonds. Satia had to clamp her hands over her mouth to stop a laugh.

Mosango, who was trying to stand despite being shoved around, froze and stared at Gneech and Satia openmouthed. Behind him, Dugadee raised the whip again, only to receive the blunt end of Gneech's staff right in his gut. Satia dug her dagger out of her boot, the tarry sludge sticking the blade in its sheath for an uncomfortable instant. Once it was out, Satia ran forward and cut the rope holding Mosango prisoner. The old man fell back with eyes wide, nodding to her as she turned to cut Septimus away from the pole holding him. The boy fell with a grunt, writhing on the ground, and Satia knelt to try to cut his arms free of the bonds. His ropes were thicker, the knots tighter. Obviously, he'd fought a lot more than the old man.

While Satia struggled with Septimus's bonds, Mosango took off like a shot, picking up the long stick that Urgo had been using on Septimus and holding it like a sword. He let out a rusty battle cry and cracked Dugadee upside the head with it, snapping the hobgoblin around in a complete circle. Beside Satia, Urgo managed a yell that was half roar, half squawk, dragging a sword from his belt and shoving her over before she could slice all the way through the rope at Septimus's wrist. Her knife skittered from her hand to bump against Urgo's boot, and he stepped on it with a wide-toothed grin. Then came his backhand, cracking as sharply as Dugadee's whip.

Urgo's slap knocked her across the chamber, and she splatted into the wall. Septimus spun about, kicking at Urgo viciously, but the hobgoblin laughed. Urgo reached out and slapped one hand on top of Septimus's head. He shoved the boy back with an easy push, toppling Septimus to the ground. The black-haired boy writhed on the floor, trying to get his feet back under him as Satia darted in to punch Urgo. Urgo danced back, and she chased him, swinging wildly in anger. Using the opening, Satia raced toward her lost dagger, but almost tripped in shock as she saw something completely unexpected going on in the hallway nearby—Gneech was *dancing.*

Satia froze midswing, staring at Gneech as the goblin twisted and wiggled right in the middle of the combat. What on Krynn was he *doing?* Chanting and shaking his staff, all the little baubles clacking back and forth amid the rags, the goblin was completely entranced with his movements. He stomped his feet, shook his arms, and sung rhythmically in some odd goblin tongue, his eyes bugging out with the effort of it. Something flickered around the goblin's fingers, a faint misty smoke rising up beneath his fingernails. Gneech's forehead crinkled up, his eyes narrowed to slivers, and he stomped his feet even harder—back and forth, back and forth. Whatever he was doing, it'd better happen soon, Satia thought, or the little goblin was going to tear himself in half.

Behind Gneech, Satia could see Mosango attacking Dugadee with the stick, swinging from the side like an old soldier. He was clearly rusty, his movements slow but precise. Old dogs might not learn new tricks, but they didn't forget their first ones either, Satia figured. Dugadee fought with the cracking whip in one hand, using the filthy claws of the other to jab at Mosango, but that stick darted back and forth each time, rapping the hobgoblin on the knuckles.

Maybe if she got her dagger, she could get the ogre's attention. Satia dashed along the wall as quickly as she could, trying to find where her dagger had gone. Spotting the bright metal against the stone, Satia dived toward it.

Urgo lifted Septimus by his bound arms, shaking the boy like a toy and laughing. Septimus kicked again, but only managed a glancing blow, easily absorbed by the hobgoblin's boots. "What you doin', little fishie? Tryin' to find your girlfriend? Here she is!" Urgo jerked Septimus by the hair and the arms, carrying him toward Satia—and blocking her path to the knife.

Satia waited until the middle of his pace, when Urgo stood on only one foot, and then kicked as hard as she could. The hobgoblin tilted slightly—she wasn't *that* strong—and bent forward to regain his balance. With a bound, Satia planted one foot on Urgo's bent shoulders and launched herself over the hobgoblin toward her dagger. Flipping head over heels, Satia landed with the agility of a cat—and had enough time to plant her boot right in Urgo's stunned backside, pitching him over too.

She swept up the dagger, the hilt reassuring and cold against her palm. With a lunge, she sawed away the knots holding Septimus's arms. Even as Urgo lumbered up from the floor, Satia used the time to cut hastily through the thick rope that bound him elbow to wrist.

"All right, Urgo," Satia growled while Septimus rolled to his feet. She faced the hobgoblin. "Let's try this again."

Just then, Gneech's wiggly spell went off. A nasty, choking smoke poured from the goblin's thin-fingered hand like a coil of snakes suddenly exploding out of his palm. The multicolored smoke tendrils writhed forward, churning together as the spell rushed toward Dugadee's face. It slammed into him, the coiling smoke wrapping from ear to ear. The spell clung to him like an oddly knitted cap, and Gneech spat on the floor vindictively.

Dugadee shrieked, dropping his whip and clawing about wildly. The unexpected action caught Mosango by surprise. Dugadee got one hand on the stick, the other on Mosango's arm and wrenched. Something inside the old man's shoulder snapped, and Mosango muffled a stanched cry. He shuddered and grabbed Dugadee's wrist, but he didn't have the strength to break the hobgoblin's grasp.

Satia spun around and left Urgo to Septimus, then plunged her dagger into Dugadee's side. The hobgoblin shoved her away, but let go of Mosango to do it. Satia pulled out her dagger and stabbed a second time as Mosango crawled away. The old knight picked up his stick again with one hand, clearly unwilling to give up the fight. He lifted it, wincing, but the wound forced his arm down again. Mosango reddened with embarrassment.

Meanwhile, Septimus launched himself onto Urgo with the fury of a demon. The boy's outrage and absolute hate for captivity gave him amazing strength, and it was clear he'd thrown away all of his practice at being human and reverted to the lessons of dragonkind: to bite, claw, and tear. Urgo stumbled under the onslaught and fell once more.

Satia ducked under Dugadee's flailing arms, the black blood of her opponent staining her hands. She could tell that he wasn't badly injured by her attacks, but the wounds slowed him. Still, Dugadee was continuing to fight. Gauging his movement until she found an opening, Satia punched him in the kidney. The much taller hobgoblin bent over with a shout of pain. The wispy cloud of Gneech's magic hovered right before Dugadee's face, a wonderful target for her malice. She could hear Gneech's laughter as Dugadee stumbled. She chased him around the narrow hallway, boxing his ears while Gneech howled in amusement.

Finally, as the last of the clouds left Dugadee's

bloodshot eyes and runny nose, Satia took the hilt of her dagger and slammed the blunt end into the soft spot at the back of Dugadee's head, where the skull met the neck. The tall hobgoblin fell beneath her like a ton of bricks, unconscious.

"Can we rip out their throats?" The voice sounded too loud in the suddenly silent passageway. Satia looked up at Mosango and Septimus, who stood over the unconscious Urgo. Septimus strolled over to her and toed Dugadee with a particularly vicious kick. His sleeve had been ripped away, arm and shoulder marked with a long wound that dripped blackish blood. Septimus didn't even seem to notice.

"Can't kill 'em," Gneech burbled, stamping his staff on the ground and glaring. "Kill 'em, their friends kill Howlback prisoners. So we leave 'em alive. Drag 'em into the privy. Gotta get moving down into the keep's storage pits or we'll be found."

Septimus grumbled predictably, and Mosango patted his shoulder. Surprisingly, the boy jumped away as if resisting the touch, and scrambled over their fallen enemies. Satia and Septimus grabbed one unconscious hobgoblin while Mosango helped Gneech move the other. Together, they dragged them into the small privy room, using the rope scraps to tie their hands together. Gneech stuffed some of the dirty rags that had bound his feet into their mouths so they couldn't call for help, and Satia almost pitied Urgo and Dugadee.

"I didn't know you goblins could fight like that," Septimus said, staring at her. "You were really something else."

"Thanks," Satia said, needled. She tried to wipe some of the sewer guck from her face and shook out her curly black hair as much as possible. "But I'm not a goblin. Don't you recognize me, Septimus?"

He stared for a moment, sniffing the air confusedly. Then his eyes widened in shock. "Satia?"

CHAPTER TEN

Washing in the pools of water at the bottom of the keep's storage pits—a nice way to say "deep places where the ogres threw stuff"—got most of the gunk off Satia's clothes and allowed the small group a chance to rest and hide from their captors. "How do you know the keep so well, Gneech?" Satia asked quietly, aware that her voice would carry in the oddly shaped cave.

They were at the bottom of a rounded cave, with small pools of water burbling up from the cracked stone floor. An extra strong rope ladder hung from the top of the storage pit, about 20 feet above, down to a ledge, to another ledge, and then to the cavern floor. Swaying above them were large nets bolted to the stone walls. The ogres and hobgoblins of the keep kept their provisions in these. Massive barrels of rum and syrup, bags of grain, bushels of corn, as well as rough sheets of unworked leather and other such materials hid the group from prying eyes—so long as they were quiet. Mosango even found a sword, which replaced the pole he'd taken off Dugadee. They risked a single fluttering candle under the thickest of the nets, illuminating a mere three-foot circle that became their campground. Gneech warmed a small leather cup of some foul-smelling herbal liquid over it, muttering to himself in Goblin. Satia knelt by the side of a small pool, washing out her shoes and socks and splashing water on her tunic until the worst of the filth from the sewer rinsed away.

"When the hobgoblins took the Howlback, I followed them here. I know stories of keep, from long ago. Told from druid to druid among the Howlback in the sacred tales. Keep was once called Glorygate Keep. Now nothing but Grimegate Keep, dark and filled with mud. *Pfaugh!*" Gneech spat on the floor with so much vigor that it made Mosango jump. Septimus glared at the old man, and Mosango blushed in the candlelight and settled back down onto his seat by the cold pool. Gneech crumbled a trinket that had been hanging from the crossbar on his staff—something Satia could have sworn was a dead mouse.

"Was home to Irda—very ancient, magical beings. Used it as a watch post. Dunno what they were watching for. So the stories say, this place used to be beautiful.

Waterfall climbed down mountain like nimble goat, and keep stood proud in light of dawn, glistening with white stone." Gneech sketched it in the air so fluidly that Satia could almost see the image. "Then the Irda left. Dunno why. Maybe they were driven out. Maybe they had nothing left to stay for. Maybe the gods tell them, 'Go, get out.' Old tales say only that the Irda left behind their greatest treasure. Buried it beneath the keep.

"Now ogres control keep—Ogre King. Very bad. But worse, Dragon Highlord Thordane. Much worse. Here, drink this." He shoved the cup toward Mosango with a pitying stare. "It heal your wound."

"Can't you use a spell for that, like you did to hurt Dugadee?" Septimus asked reluctantly, turning his nose away from the horrible smell. Mosango looked at the steaming cup uneasily, licking his lips in wary preparation.

Gneech smiled viciously. "No." He waited until Mosango choked down the foul-smelling brew, eyeing every drop as it passed the old man's lips. "There. Now you feel better soon." Gneech twiddled his fingers and chuckled while Mosango coughed wildly. Satia wasn't sure if the goblin cast some silent spell on Mosango or if his horrible drink had done its job, but the wound on Mosango's arm seemed less severe, the blood less thick.

Satia and Mosango exchanged glances. This goblin could *heal*. Mosango rubbed his shoulder, wiping the blood away with a handful of water, but said nothing, eyes wide. Septimus shrugged and tore into a chunk of dried apple that Gneech handed him, noticing nothing out of line. Of course he didn't, Satia reminded herself. The dragons always had Takhisis—or Paladine. They never lost their gods or had to do without magical healing. "Strange."

"What you say?" Gneech craned his flat face around to look at her with glittering eyes.

"If the Irda left their treasure somewhere around here," Satia quickly extemporized, "why haven't the ogres found it?"

"Ogres dumb. They dig out the grounds so much they make the quarry. Then, when Highlord come, they tell him why." Gneech smiled his strange pointed smile again. "Now he not leave."

"That's why they're still digging up the mud quarry—partly to make money, but partly to search for the Irda treasure," Mosango said, tugging at his long beard. Now that it was clean of the mud for the first time, Satia could see it had a lot more brown in it than she had thought, but he was still not a young man. Scars crisscrossed his chest beneath the ragged tunic.

"Are you sure it exists?" she asked.

"Howlback clan price, ten steel a head." Gneech's shoulders drooped. "I hope Irda treasure exists, for tribe's sake. Hard to be tribe druid when you don't have tribe. Nobody to listen to old stories, nobody to drink the rotgort on moon-dark nights or dance on bog hill over enemy's bones." Gneech sighed, a sound that resembled the rumble of a stone down a loose hill. "So I find treasure. Then I buy tribe's freedom." He paused to poke at the dangling bits hanging along the crossbar of his staff, idly making them dance and swing. A strange, longing look crossed his face, but was gone as quickly as the shadow of the candle's flicker.

"So to find the treasure, they dig?" Septimus asked.

"Dig for generations. Then mountain collapse, then they dig again. Make pits like this." Gneech gestured around them at the stone walls, then up at the swaying nets. "Then start over somewhere else."

"That's stupid. If they can't find it, it isn't here. They should go find a hoard of their own." Septimus bristled at the thought. "Just like you should find another tribe. This one's stupid. They got caught."

Gneech shot him a dark look. "Careful, boy," he said. "Maybe you get hurt next time, and I make drink with wrong things in it."

"Easy now," Mosango said, quickly stepping in

between the sharp, sudden glares. "No one's being left behind—not the Howlback, and not your mother either, Septimus."

The reminder caught Septimus sharply, and the boy snarled. He glanced toward Satia as if gauging something, then relaxed. "Of course not. Nobody gets left behind, Mosango. Nobody at all." Satia could tell there was something more to their conversation, from the evil tone underlying Septimus's words to the paling of Mosango's face behind his long, bushy beard. The old knight cleared his throat and looked away.

What was *that* about?

"So." Satia stepped in, wringing water from her short, dark curls. "All we have to do is free Septimus's mother, and then either defeat all the ogres, hobgoblins and draconians, or find the Irda treasure and buy the Howlback's freedom. The treasure chamber might even have something we can use to free Septimus's mother, some kind of magic item or weapon. Then we can all leave." She sat down on a rock beside Mosango and shook out her watery boots.

"Great. Sounds easy," Septimus said without much conviction.

"I've done more difficult things on adventures back at home." The lie just slipped out without her even thinking about it. Satia felt herself color, and quickly turned to Gneech before anyone could ask uncomfortable questions. "How well do you know the keep? Is there any part of it you haven't searched?"

The goblin shrugged lumpily. "Searched it wherever I ended up. Saw throne room. Deep pits below main areas of fort. Many passages, above and below, some blocked, some open. Areas where rocks have filled in hallways, where you can't go past the stones. Treasure could be trapped in collapsed chambers. Could be in secret treasure room somewhere in keep. Dunno. I know keep pretty well. Never find it." He paused. "Maybe have some ideas, though." The goblin eyed them thoughtfully. "Might involve digging."

"What did you have in mind?" Mosango asked, leaning forward. He spoke a bit too eagerly, the sound of his voice echoing uncomfortably through the pit. Satia hushed the old man. When it quieted down again, Mosango continued. "You've got an advantage that you didn't have before—us."

"There is passage down at bottom of pit, near center of keep," Gneech began slowly, spreading his thin-fingered hands and sketching in the air again to draw a crude map. "Passage I never explore. Ogres never explore because they never find. Broke open few months ago during rock slide. Rock is smooth there, smooth like glass all along the wall. Floor is bright there, like painted glass. Very strange. Old. I look down in it, I don't see myself—I see through glass floor and water runs below. I try to use passage as another way to dungeons, but I never make it."

"Why not?" Satia leaned forward. She was able to visualize the passage, so well did the goblin druid describe it.

"Monster," Gneech said simply. "At least one. Maybe more. Didn't stop to count. I just ran."

Satia, Mosango, and Septimus looked at each other. "Do you think there's a good chance that leads to a treasure chamber?" Mosango finally asked.

"Maybe. Lots of traps down there. Usually people don't trap things that aren't worth finding." Gneech's logic seemed foolproof.

"If the traps are still working and this monster was still down there, then nobody else has been past that site successfully," Satia reasoned. "If that is where the treasure was, it's very likely that whatever was there is still there." The others nodded, Septimus eagerly, Gneech sagely, Mosango as if he were gravely concerned.

"It will be dangerous," the old knight warned them. "The Knights of Solamnia tell tales of these 'Irda,' but the stories are very, very old—and I don't know how accurate they are. The tales say they were a magical race, the forebearers of the ogres. Cruel, beautiful, and very powerful. That's most of what I know of them, but it is enough to tell us all that if they truly owned this keep and created that treasure room, then it will be difficult indeed."

"We can do it." Septimus paced back and forth behind them with an inexhaustible supply of energy. "Gneech knows the way, and he has magic. Mosango knows about the Irda . . . well, more than any of us!"

"I know how to find traps. I did it in Gwynned. In the sewers." Satia bit her lip as both Mosango and Septimus stared at her disbelievingly. "I'm telling the truth!" she blurted out, clenching her fists.

"Your father, the prince, had you picking locks and finding traps?" Septimus hissed cruelly. "I believe *that*."

Mosango didn't seem to find it any more credible. "I thought you said your father was a merchant who worked for the prince. Why would he let his daughter go into the sewers?" Without realizing it, the crazy old knight wrinkled his nose like a dog smelling something foul. "Satia, you're not making sense."

Standing, Satia half yelled, "My father was a thief in Gwynned. I don't even know his name. My mother died when I was three, and the orphanage took me in. I've lived in the streets and sewers all my life, and I know how to do this. You have to trust me. If anyone can make sure we get through there safely, it's me."

"How can we believe you? A while ago, you were a princess, then a rich merchant's daughter, and now you're an accomplished thief?" Mosango wobbled his hands back and forth in confusion. "It doesn't make any sense."

Crossing her arms defensively, Satia tried to keep the hot tears from showing. "I'm telling the truth."

"Maybe." Septimus snorted.

It was Gneech, the wizened goblin, who stuck up for her. "Girl has good head on her shoulders. Went into filthy river to save friends." He poked Mosango's chest with a gnarled, twiglike finger. "You." Gneech rounded on Septimus with a glare that would make any dragon proud. "Got trapped under a rock slide trying to save friends too. Maybe you don't remember that, eh? Me, I think girl's earned a little trust, even if she stretches the truth now and then." Mosango and Septimus both fell silent at the goblin's harsh words, the knight's eyes sliding along the damp floor of the cavern. "And I think maybe girl not the only one with something in her past she's ashamed of. Right, old man?"

Mosango jumped as if stung. Septimus threw him the same nasty stare he'd been giving Satia. "Hey, yeah.

What was Urgo talking about back there, Mosango? The part about selling your armor and how you killed some boy." Satia stared blankly at the boy, unsure whether to be glad that the goblin convinced them to trust her, or concerned about whatever Mosango had done. Gneech shrugged, uninterested in the details, and started idly tightening the rags on his staff. Mosango reddened up to his ears.

Mosango shook his head fiercely. "Nothing. It's not important."

"The hobgoblins seemed to think it was," Septimus countered. "And if it's not, then you can tell us about it. Right?" The little dragon-boy stomped his foot in a decent approximation of an impatient toddler. "So explain. They said you were drinking. They said you sold your armor, and they said—"

This time, it was Mosango who interrupted Septimus. "Stop!" he cried. "Stop!" The old man put his hands over his ears, sinking down over his knees in his seat on the stone. "I'll tell you."

All eyes turned to the man as he lowered his hands to tug on his long gray beard. When he spoke again, his voice was dimmer, as if he were repeating a story that had been told to him long ago.

"I was a Knight of Solamnia. I have told you that, and it is true. I once rode the great dragons through the skies in the fight against Takhisis, not so long ago. And I had a squire, a young boy named Loris. He was very dear to me. And he . . . he died." Clearing his throat, Mosango rose from his seat, wrapping his arms around himself as he spoke dully. "Everything after that is a blur. I drank," he admitted. "Heavily. My friends in Solamnia began to lose touch with me. I would have been thrown out of the order, save for the pity of a few friends I still had among the knights.

"The order sent me away on a useless mission. I knew it was only to get rid of me. They were as ashamed of me . . . as I was of myself." Mosango raised his eyes to the casks hanging above him in the nets, a sudden longing entering his eyes. He cleared his throat uncomfortably and continued. "I started taking on adventures—anything I could find, no matter how dangerous. If I couldn't complete them, couldn't defeat the monster threatening the village or rescue the hostages, I'd just leave and go somewhere else. Eventually, I found my way into the bog. I had no money and even less self-respect.

"I sold my armor to Thordane. I always kept it perfect—it was a magnificent set. I've seen him wearing it. Steel, gold, and ebony." It took Mosango a minute to come out of his reverie. "Is that what you wanted to know, Septimus?"

Before the glaring boy could answer, Mosango fell to his knees and put his hands on Septimus's shoulders. "I would never let anything happen to you. You are a dragon, a noble creature of the sky, and I . . . I'm sworn to work with you, as a knight. I still remember that vow." The earnest look on Mosango's wrinkled, careworn face was almost fanatical, consuming him. He shook Septimus lightly to emphasize the point. "Tell me that you accept my oath."

"Mosango, Septimus isn't your squire," Satia said hesitantly. She was afraid to contradict the old man. The strange passion on his face, the way he clutched at Septimus as if the boy were his last hope—that scared her.

"I know that." He didn't even look at her, his eyes locked on the boy's. "He's a dragon. And we made our oaths to Huma and to Paladine. It's another chance, at last, to redeem myself in Paladine's eyes through one of his most noble servants."

Gneech was staring at them with his strange, flat eyes. He let out a little giggle, muffling it against his rag-wrapped stick. Satia had a feeling that Gneech had seen what kind of dragon Thordane and his men captured, and that it was about as much one of Paladine's noble servants as it was a bog leech. She opened her mouth to say something, but Septimus was quicker.

"Sure." The boy said simply with a shrug. Satia could have killed him.

Mosango looked as though he'd been touched by Paladine. He lifted Septimus and swung him about in a display of strength she wouldn't have thought possible from Mosango's withered form. He held the boy close for a moment and then set him back on the ground. "Thank you. Thank you. You won't regret it. I'll protect you. I'll make sure you have a tale to tell your mother and the other dragons of Krynn that will rival Huma. You will find me your most dedicated servant."

She knew that she had to tell Mosango the truth, but when she opened her mouth to say something, she got a quick elbow jab to the ribs from the goblin. "You tell him now," the wise little druid hissed, "you break his heart and maybe his mind too. He break like twig in river, and where will we be? Not better, you bet on that. Old man find out in time. Be better for it too."

She was just going to have to trust that Gneech was right. Satia deflated, saving one particularly nasty look for Septimus, who preened under Mosango's attention. "Can we get going?" she asked through clenched teeth. "I don't want to stay here much longer. Something might find us." She flared her nostrils and stared at Septimus. "Something horrible, and awful, and deceitful, and wicked and altogether vile." He just grinned back at her, and when Mosango wasn't watching, he stuck his thumbs in his ears and waggled his fingers.

"You forgot filthy," Septimus whispered as they followed Gneech toward the ladder out of the pit. He sniffed at her thoughtfully. "Too bad you don't have time for another bath." Oddly, after the boy's accusations earlier, his teasing seemed almost . . . friendly.

Septimus marched to the ladder and scurried up, following in Gneech's footsteps. The goblin was the fastest climber of them all, vanishing over the lip of the pit long before agile Septimus could get halfway up the ladder. She watched the boy, his chest puffed out in pride, convinced that he was victorious over them all. How she hated his arrogance, his snarky voice, and his strut. He didn't deserve this—and still he was winning.

"You don't have to understand him." The soft voice at her elbow was Mosango. She started, unaware that the old knight had been standing so close. He, too, was staring up at the scurrying boy, watching him climb from net to net and then up the last of the rope ladders into the pit. "You can't understand him, in fact, so don't even try. He isn't human, even if he looks like it. Even if he knows how to act like it."

"He acted like it pretty darn well back in Gwynned," Satia remembered.

126

"Dragons learn masks from an early age, and remember, Septimus is probably a century old, despite his appearance. He's a child—but a child among dragons." Mosango smiled.

"You seem to know a lot about them," Satia said curiously.

"I spent a great deal of time with them in Solamnia during the War of the Lance. My dragon, Gleamfire, was one of my closest friends. Dragons learn unlike any other creature I've ever encountered, memorizing huge amounts of information by rote, learning even as they dream. They are cunning down to the last, and brave. They are a species so far beyond us that our petty arguments must seem strange and meaningless to him." Mosango's eyes were alight with that weird hero worship again. "How can we hope to understand them?"

"I dunno. Maybe by asking questions?"

Mosango apparently was too far gone to recognize sarcasm when he heard it. "Perhaps. But Septimus is too young to tell us much. His mother, though—what a magnificent creature she must be! Gold . . . or silver, perhaps. Definitely noble, you can tell as much from his bearing." Before she could spit out her distaste, Mosango spun to face her. "Satia, I have to thank you. Without your bravery helping him this far, I never would have had this chance . . . this opportunity to

redeem myself, to put my squire's soul to rest at last."
He placed his hand on her shoulder. "Thank you."

It was about the last thing she wanted him to
say, the last thing she wanted to hear. Thank you?
For bringing that terror here? For lying to them every
chance she got just to make sure they wouldn't laugh
at her? For letting Septimus take advantage of the mad
old man's personal problems? Maybe he meant "thank
you for giving me the opportunity to be Nox's lunch,"
but as they hadn't met Nox yet, perhaps that one was
premature. She just nodded, unable to speak past the
lump in her throat.

Mosango climbed up the rope ladder toward the
top of the pit, where she could see Septimus doing a
self-satisfied jig far above her. She clutched the ropes
to pull herself up after Mosango. She had only one
thought on her mind.

Sooner or later, she was going to turn that little
snot over her knee, dragon or no dragon.

CHAPTER ELEVEN

"Ssssh!" Gneech hissed, pausing as he climbed over a fallen mass of rock within a deep corridor. He turned toward them, the light from the candle pasted on top of his head shining eerily into his eyes. "Must walk silently now. This bad place. Very bad. But only way to secret passages deep below keep."

"What's wrong, Gneech?" Satia ventured, choking back the rest of her words when she saw Gneech's nasty glare.

"Ssssh!" he hissed again, stamping his foot silently on the stone. When they were all quiet, the goblin pointed upward. His whisper echoed in the stillness of the passage. "Great Hall just above." A cold chill ran down Satia's spine. The Great Hall? The room where Nox was being held captive, probably where Thordane kept his throne and the two young dragons that served him? She gulped.

"Yes," Gneech whispered. "You see problem. One

sound, and they will hear us. No matter what you hear or see, we must be like mice in the walls."

The goblin fixed his stern gaze on Septimus. "That means especially *you*. You see mother, you smell mother, you no call to her. All that will do is get us caught. We get caught, we lose. Mother never be free. You understand?"

Biting his lip, Septimus paused, nostrils flaring. Could he already smell his mother's scent on the wind? Satia didn't know how acute the boy's senses were in this human form. He scowled. "I get it."

Gneech nodded and moved forward down the partially collapsed passage, taking great care with each footstep not to move any loose earth. He paused as they followed, watching to see that they did the same, and gave Mosango a particularly fierce snarl when the old man kicked loose a stone.

Each step was slow and careful, and Satia even tried to lessen her breathing so that the hiss of each exhalation wouldn't echo in the air. Gneech put out his candle, and in the darkness Satia could see thin shafts of light drifting down from the crumbling stone above. Septimus froze, looking up, a strange, frightened exultation in his eyes.

And then Satia heard it—the shifting of thousands of pounds of weight across stone moorings somewhere up above, in the room. There was a deep breath, hundreds of times larger than her own, and the hiss of a serpent's coils shifting against one another. Although Gneech continued onward carefully and silently, Satia couldn't help herself. She pulled herself up onto one of the crumbled piles of stone and pressed her eye to the crack just above.

Through the hole in the stone, Satia could see a large room, vast by comparison to all the places she knew. The main chamber of Grimegate Keep still held a faint touch of the ancient glory it once knew, from the almost impossibly smooth stone that made its walls, to the stained-glass windows with their fading colors struggling to catch the kiss of the sun. The ceiling was high and arched, with buttresses made of black glass that looked as though smoke held the roof aloft.

But even with all that, it was very apparent that the keep had fallen on hard times. From her angle at what appeared to be at the foot of a corner of the room, Satia could see that the floor was patched and stained, frayed wood nailed slipshod over holes that must lead into the corridors beneath. The grimy walls had holes where hooks must have once been attached to the stone to hold tapestries—but now even the hook itself was absent, and the wall was bare. The worst of the damage was easy to see: a huge section of the roof in the south corner had fallen in, the edges supported by ramshackle columns. Through the cleft, the forms of orangey-red scaled draconians hovered and wheeled, barely able to keep aloft. They were unwieldy in flight, their thick leather armor unbalancing them, and they were already poor at flying without all that to encumber them. Some perched on the columns or the edges of the roof. They sharpened their weapons, cleaned their armor, and snarled down at the hobgoblins in the quarries below, like strange brassy crows.

There was a set of wide, evenly spaced stone stairs against the north wall of the room, the top one wide enough to be a dais, but the throne that had been placed there was little more than a big chair draped in thick, gold velvet curtains. Clean and well kept, it looked strange in the throne room that was otherwise falling apart.

But the most eye-catching thing in the room, of course, was the dragon.

She was massive, her head so much larger than the throne that she could have swallowed it whole. Her black scales were so dark they absorbed the light and glistened from snout to tail tip, white fangs gleaming against her black lips. She lay with her head outstretched over razor-sharp claws, golden eyes open just a slit, watching everything. Only the tip of her long tail moved, flinching impatiently back and forth. Her thick, furled wings were coiled against her catlike body, and a ruff of hornlets extended from the back of her head and along her jaw. From one end to the other, the great dragon was nearly forty feet in length. A greenish stain of scarred flesh marred the perfect obsidian of her skin. It coiled about one leg from her ankle to the base of her wing and looked like an old wound that had healed long ago.

A thick collar of strange, shimmering iron had been sealed around her neck, which was marked with scratches where she'd tested its strength. A chain of darker, even more stalwart material stretched and coiled past her shoulder, trickling along the floor to a hook on the back wall. Nox's eyes occasionally flicked to it with a hateful attitude, then away again, as if unwilling to be caught staring at the magic that bound her.

"Wow," Satia breathed, frozen. Behind her, one of her companions tugged silently at her hand, but she didn't even turn around to see who it was.

Dwarfed by the black dragon's bulk, two small red dragons curled around the throne. Now that Satia had seen Nox, the Reds looked like toys, barely larger than horse-sized creatures with a definite puppylike quality to their movements. Clumsy and grumpy, the two small dragons snapped at one another playfully, settling down only for a short time before provoking one another again. Those must be the two baby red dragons that Thordane was raising. Vex and Beset, she remembered Thordane calling them.

The wide door where two ogre guards stood swung open suddenly, and the guards tried to stand straighter despite their hunched spines and unbalanced arms. The human who walked through was much smaller than the ogres despite his bulky plate-mail armor. The armor was magnificent, steel trimmed in gold and black, and a long golden cloak of fine material swooped around his shoulder and over one arm. He carried a stag-antlered helm in one hand, a perpetual self-satisfied sneer marring the otherwise perfect features of his face. He had golden hair, and his golden beard was trimmed close like a nobleman's. Only his dark, dark eyes betrayed the pure, malicious evil in his soul.

Thordane arranged himself on the velvet-covered throne, reaching down to pet Vex and Beset before settling his gaze on Nox. The two little dragons licked playfully at his hand as they might a parent, but something in their eyes told Satia that they were only as loyal as they were cowed. If Thordane ever failed in front of them or looked weak, they might revert to their wild, evil natures and tear the human apart in the blink of an eye. Satia considered that for a moment, until Thordane's voice broke the silence.

"Care for a fly today, my dear?" he asked Nox in a sugary tone. In response, the great black dragon allowed a little drool to slip out between her fangs. It ran along her lip and fell to the floor. Where it struck, it boiled and hissed, the acid searing through the stone.

Thordane laughed. "That's no way to treat your new partner, Nox. Not when I've been so generous to you—and in Takhisis's name!" Vex and Beset echoed Thordane's laughter with abrupt, chuffing sounds.

Nox raised her head a few inches from the stone. "You have no right to claim my partnership in that name, human," she snarled. Her voice sounded like the deep bellows of the earth, rolling and boiling in her belly. She snapped toward him, jaws closing on the air just short of his throne. "She has long ago forgotten me, and it is best that she has."

"I know your history, Nox. You did not come when the Dark Queen called her dragons to battle. You are a traitor to her—or worse, a coward. I doubt she'd care if you were"—Thordane smiled—"mistreated."

"She might destroy me for my insolence, yes. But for you, a human who dares capture one of her dragons, destruction would be far from her mind. My queen is not known for being merciful." Nox's eyes were cold, the words hissing out past her teeth with a burst of sulfurous breath. Thordane's cloak shivered about the legs of his throne, and he pretended to ponder.

"Best she not hear of it, then, until we have delivered her a victory that she cannot ignore. Takhisis may not be merciful, but she is practical. If I can destroy a stronghold of her enemies, then I think she will be willing to reevaluate the situation." His smile was cold. "Think on it, Nox. Together, we could begin the war once more, pick up where Takhisis was forced to stop."

"Release me, fool. I will have no part of your plan. Suicide. If you did not have my child . . ." Acid lashed from her teeth as she spat out the words, splashing out toward Thordane. He leaned back and smiled, and the acid veered in the air around him, splattering the floor of the dais. So that's why Nox was being so calm—she thought Thordane already had Septimus captive! Satia took in a sharp breath.

An elbow jammed into her side, and the air came out of her lungs in a rush. "Scoot over," Septimus hissed. "I want to see my mother." Grudgingly, Satia shared the view.

Thordane smiled. "Now, now, Nox. This armor was made by the Solamnic Knights for battle against creatures such as you. I took it from a knight who cared more for wine than for glory." Thordane laughed, and Satia winced, glancing back over her shoulder to where Gneech was helping Mosango crawl over a hill of collapsed stone. "I do not fear you, Nox," Thordane continued. "Were you not as strong as you are, the power of that collar would not only prohibit your spellcasting, it would also bend you to my will. I am pleased that you fight against it. I would not wish for a partner who was . . . weak. Furthermore, my spells are strong enough that your breath cannot hurt me."

The ogres by the door had had no such protection, though. As Nox tried her acid breath again, the acid sloshed around them. One screamed, leaping away with smoking boots, and the other, not as quick, found himself on fire in spots from the sulfurous gunk. After he hurriedly beat out the flames with his partner's cloak, the second ogre turned and fled down the hallway with a howl of terror.

Speaking the language of magic, Thordane unleashed a mighty bolt of force that arced from his hand to Nox's head. It cracked against her jaw, snapping it shut before she could complete her acidic spew. Wild sparks of power snapped about her face, blinding her temporarily. In a rare burst of temper, the wizard raised his voice. "YOU WILL OBEY!"

Nox let out an infuriated roar to match Thordane's command. "If it weren't for this chain . . ." Nox threatened, lashing her head about to free it from the spell. With a small, satisfied smile, Thordane released the spell and the sparks faded.

"I'd still have your son." Thordane reached into a small pouch at his side and drew out a tuft of black hair. He rolled it between his fingers as the lightning flashes cleared from Nox's vision. Thordane reached out to rub Vex's jaw, and the little red dragon purred deep within his throat. Beset hissed and snapped at the air jealously, then was silenced by a whisper from Thordane. "Dragons don't reproduce easily, do they?" the wizard asked idly. "It seems to me that was the entire focus of Takhisis's original plan to keep the good dragons out of the War of the Lance. Attack their eggs— the children of the beasts. Dragons will do anything for their children. It's your nature, good or bad." His eyes flicked up to her arrogantly, and he tossed the little clump of jet black hair at her feet.

"I have your child, Nox." Thordane sat back in his throne. "And thus . . . I have you."

"Not if I can help it," Septimus snarled. He drew in a great breath of air, bracing himself to yell out to his mother, but Satia punched him in the stomach, forcing the boy to choke back his cry.

"Stop it!" she hissed, shaking him by the shoulders. "If they know we're here, they'll capture us!"

"If she knows I'm free—" he started, but Satia interrupted him.

"You won't *stay* free if they find out we're in here, and that's the important part. What are you going to do? Yell, 'Hey, Mom, I'm over here,' and then apologize when they drag you in front of her in chains?" Satia met his black eyes unflinchingly with her own, holding him in an intense stare. "Don't waste your freedom."

"Your Lordship?" A new voice, low and growly, came suddenly from the chamber above. Satia shoved Septimus back and peered through the crack again. A yellow-skinned ogre, larger than the others, stood in the archway, carrying the limp form of the ogre guard who had fled. This ogre had patched together a set of chain and plate armor from scraps that were obviously too small for him. He'd painted the lot of it a sterling blue that clashed horribly with his yellow skin. A long topknot of green hair stuck out from the top of his head in a rude approximation of a knight's flowing helm ornamentation. "You need a new door guard." He dropped the unconscious ogre on the floor by the doorway.

"Yes, it seems that I do, Zargut." The Highlord tapped his fingers on the arm of the throne, eying the ogres warily. "You have news?"

"Who is that?" Satia wondered softly.

Gneech tried to drag her from her perch as he whispered, "Ogre King. Very bad. Come, we must go now." But Satia couldn't help looking back to see more of the scene.

Zargut glanced at the dragon prowling beside the Highlord's chair and straightened his stance. "Yes, my lord. There was a collapse in the quarries this morning. Only one dead prisoner, but it will slow our work by a few days to clear the stone out of the mud." Satia noticed that unlike other ogres, this one had taken great pains to speak Common clearly. He was clean too, and his teeth were more white than yellow.

"Work them through the night tonight, Zargut. Tell your ogres and the hobgoblins to spare no lash." Thordane seemed bored by all this, as if the news meant little to him. "So long as we meet the quotas and continue to make money, I don't care if we lose a few workers. We'll just find more." He turned back to his dragons, but the ogre shifted in front of the throne, reluctant to leave.

"My lord?" Zargut was clearly uncertain about continuing. "There is some advantageous news as well."

"Speak," Thordane snapped, settling down once more into his throne.

"We have discovered a series of passages beneath the keep, untouched since the time of the Irda. This may be the key to recovering the lost treasures. Those passages may lead to chambers, and one of those may be the trove beneath my keep. The sword—"

"*Your* keep?" Thordane turned his irritation to the well-spoken ogre. "Don't you mean *my* keep?"

Zargut swallowed hard, sweat breaking out on his brow. "Yes, my lord, of course. My forefathers . . . but . . . um . . . *your* keep." Appeased, Thordane nodded, and the ogre continued. "The Irda hoard must still be down there. This discovery may be the key to getting their magical treasures for your war."

"That is excellent news, Zargut." Thordane's mood was as changeable as a spring day, and he almost purred as he leaned back into his velvet-covered throne. "With powerful weapons, we can arm the hobgoblins against Solamnic forces and make our attack completely debilitating. With steel, we could buy a bigger army, equip it, overrun the fortifications on the Solamnian border. Once we have completed such a powerful strike against the knights, Takhisis will see that she must lend us her aid. The war will begin again—and we will be its heroes." Caught up in the moment, Thordane crowed,

"Takhisis will crown me in glory!"

This guy, Satia thought, was truly mad.

"Whatever the Irda left behind, we shall use it," Thordane continued. He started issuing orders. "Zargut, take two of your ogres and search the passages. If you come upon traps, take some of the goblins and use them as fodder."

"From what we've seen in other areas, there may be many traps, my lord."

Glaring, Thordane continued. "When you run out of goblins, use *ogres*. Your squeamishness will not slow down my war."

Paling, Zargut bowed. "By your will, my lord." He paused as if considering whether to test Thordane's patience, then took a half step forward and pushed his luck. "And when we find the trove, you will give me the sword then? We made a deal. The hoard is yours, no matter what we find there, but the sword belongs to me."

Thordane sighed, waving his hand dismissively. "Yes, yes, you greedy ogre. You can have the sword. A Highlord remembers his promises." Aware that he was being given a gift, Zargut fell to one knee and praised his master in puppylike tones through gritted teeth. The ogre seemed embarrassed to be doing it. Satia was certainly embarrassed for him.

"Gneech is right," she whispered softly, allowing the goblin to tug her down from the pile of rubble. "We need to hurry. If they find that treasure before we do, we'll lose everything."

"Then we can't let that happen," Septimus growled. "No matter what."

CHAPTER TWELVE

"You said it was close," Septimus whined. Gneech didn't even bother to look back, but Satia elbowed the boy when Mosango wasn't looking. She wasn't sure what the crazy old knight would think of her jabbing at the dragon that was his "last hope."

It definitely wasn't the kind of adventuring party all the books talked about, or the kind that Satia had always imagined joining. Here she was, crawling through the bowels of a dilapidated castle with a goblin, an insane Solamnic Knight, and a boy who only a few days ago had considered her lunch. Satia climbed over some fallen rocks and rubble into the passageway, muttering about how life was unfair. Her lies were better than this truth. Why was everyone getting so fussy about that?

The strange, bobbing candle on the goblin's head led them through the twisting underground passages like a weaving, drunken star.

"This is place." Gneech reached to help Satia through the broken wall.

Satia had crawled through mud pits, labored in dirt quarries, and swam sewers of unimaginable gunk. The last thing she was prepared to see was this . . . beauty. Bright mosaics tiled the corridor before her. The pattern of the chipped glass did not disguise the fact that there was a room beneath them, a deep chamber with something twinkling far beneath in the faint gleam of Gneech's little candle.

Mosango ran his hands over the walls, looking at the intricate patterns in the tiles. "Magnificent."

Satia and Septimus crouched at Gneech's feet, trying to peer down through the glass floor. The thick, solid glass held her weight easily. It was like a massive stained-glass window underfoot. It was amazing. Satia had never seen anything like it before, never even dreamed it was possible.

"Is the Irda treasure down there?" Septimus pounded a fist on the glass. "Can we break this and get down to it?"

Satia grabbed his hand. "Hey! Cut it out! If you break it, we all fall—including you. You don't have wings anymore, remember?"

He pouted, pulling his hand out of hers. "Well there's got to be some way we can get down there and check. I can't even see if there's a weapon down there to free my mother. I can't see much of anything except sort of a twinkle." Septimus smushed his cheek on the glass in his desperation to get a better view.

Mosango kneeled beside them and eyed the panels. "Even if we could fly down from this height, I don't think we could break the floor without a rock hammer and several hours' labor. It's easily a foot thick. This was designed to hold much greater weight than ours."

"So how do we get down there?" asked the boy.

"Corridor go two ways. Left . . . and right." Gneech gestured. Every time he turned his head, the light from his candle flickered and bobbed, casting strange shadows in the hallway. "We follow one way until it end, then come back, follow other. One has to lead down eventually. This castle not so big. Deep, yes, but not big." Gneech froze, sniffing the air gingerly, and lowered his voice. "Be very quiet. Smell . . . of ogre."

"You can smell ogres here?" Satia whispered. "Like, recently?"

"Yes, very recent." Gneech sniffed about the rock-slide, down the wall, trailing his fingers in the corner of the hallway like a hunting dog. He lifted a long black piece of string up with a gleam of victory in his eye. "See? Is ogre hair. Very new. Ogres also find this corridor, I think."

Mosango sobered. "Then we have to move quickly, before they find the treasure. We got lucky with those hobgoblins, but we're not ready to fight ogres." He clutched the short sword he'd stuck in his ratted belt, the same one he'd taken from the keep stores. He glanced at Satia's dagger and the sword she'd taken from Urgo, Gneech's twisted, rag-covered staff and crossbar, and then down at Septimus, who carried no weapons at all. He looked down both branches, and then made an arbitrary decision. "That way," the old knight pointed with his sword. "We go that way first."

They moved down the hallway in a slender row, one after the other, taking care to make very little sound. Satia went first, holding her dagger in one hand but leaving the sword stuck through her belt. She needed one hand for finding traps. If these beautiful corridors were indeed made by the Irda to protect their treasure trove, then it was certain that there would be traps. They might be old, but if there was one thing Satia learned working in the sewers as a thief for the Underground, it's that you never take chances on "might be." Satia snuck a glance at Mosango and hung her head a bit. They'd never understand what it'd been like down there. Without a family, without friends . . .

"Satia, are you all right?" Mosango's voice cut through her thoughts, and she realized that she'd been standing still while the others went ahead.

"I'm fine," she snapped, tugging at a curl of her dark hair and pushing past him. "Fine."

They moved slowly through the passages, backing up when they came to other areas that had collapsed under the weight of rocks, continuing forward whenever the passage looked like it headed downward. Three times, Satia stopped them and adjusted a tile on the wall or a bit of iron piping between plates of the glass floor.

"So you really can do this," Septimus sneered when she took her shaking hands away from a newly disarmed poison-dart trap.

"You didn't believe me?" she asked wryly, mopping a bit of sweat out of her eyes. He didn't answer, and neither did the others. Satia kept her eyes stubbornly on the floor, the next wall, the next trap, trying to convince herself that it didn't matter what they knew or what they thought about her. She was doing her job. They'd find a way to get the treasure and get out of here—and then go home. Let Septimus, Mosango, and Gneech think whatever they wanted about her. She didn't care.

There were traps everywhere—old ones, sigils, and strange magical percussions that Satia wasn't even sure still worked. But she didn't take a chance, disarming them or teaching the others to step around them without triggering anything. A number of them went off while she worked on them, but she survived, and the group continued onward. She successfully disarmed many more than she'd missed. Nevertheless, they made her jumpy. Just one mistake, and—

"Watch out!" Satia threw herself to the floor, covering her head with her hands as the trap she'd been working on went off. A puff of green fire exploded across the top of the hallway, singeing her hair. She heard Gneech cry out in surprise and saw Mosango dive on top of Septimus, protecting the boy from the flame. When the roar ended in a wispy, gasping hiss, Satia opened one eye and peeked above her. The ceiling and the top half of the corridor were blackened, and a fine dusting of ash trickled down. "Whoops."

Septimus shoved the old knight away with a disgusted noise, and Gneech waggled his staff by the twisted crossbar, testing to see if the ceiling was going to cave in above them. "It's not as easy as it looks," Satia said defensively, crawling to her knees. "These things are old, and they get stuck."

"That's what you said when that last blade popped out and almost cut Gneech in half," Septimus snarled. "And when the other one dumped magic snakes all over the floor."

"The snakes weren't my fault!" Satia protested. "And they vanished after just a few minutes. We didn't even have to fight them."

"Maybe you should go back to being a rich merchant's daughter." Septimus's lip curled. "You were better at that."

Gneech smacked them both in the knees with a single wide sweep of his rag-covered staff. "Enough!" he barked. "You two, always fighting! Traps are good. If we find no traps, then they had nothing to protect—or someone been here before. Traps mean this right way!" His voice raised into a screech as the little goblin beat both of them lightly with the length of his weapon. "So you both stop fighting and shut up, or the ogres will find us from you making . . . so . . . much . . ." —Gneech's staff slowly came to a frozen halt, and his wide, flat eyes peered down the corridor behind him—". . . noise. Uh-oh."

A group of ogres—a mobile mountain of muscle with ten legs and enough wooden clubs to populate a small forest—stood at the far end of the corridor behind them, quirky stares on their deadpan faces. Only one of them, a big guy whose metal armor was painted a lurid shade of sky blue, shoved his way forward until he realized what they'd found. "GET THEM!" he roared, pointing.

"RUN!" Gneech yelled back as if it were a battle cry of his own. "It's the Ogre King!" The goblin turned on his heel and fled past the girl.

Septimus planted his feet and flexed his arms as if he still had claws on every finger, ready to fight, but Mosango swept the boy off his feet and pitched down the corridor after Gneech, rushing past Satia in the blink of an eye. For a strange, uncomfortable moment, Satia stared at the confused ogres, meeting eye to eye with the big one in blue armor. She reached out quickly, before he could speak, and jabbed the trap she'd just discovered. "Oops," she said quietly before any of them could speak.

The roar of flame exploded out again, and Satia dived away from the ogres, back in the direction that Gneech and the others had fled. Gneech grabbed her shoulders to drag her along the passage even as the heat wave of the trap scattered more ash above their heads. "Good work! Only a moment now before ogres come. Must run!" He gripped her hand with iron fingers, dragging her up onto her feet. She could see Mosango ahead, still carrying Septimus over one shoulder, his sword out in the other hand.

"Gneech!" Satia protested. "We can't run this way! We haven't been down this corridor! There are going to be more traps!" She followed him unwillingly, jerked along like a puppet. "The traps will kill us before the ogres do!"

"You have better idea?" The goblin's eyes were wide and terrified, his knuckles white from clutching her hand. Looking behind them as the green flame was dying out and all five ogres plowed toward them, Satia had to admit that she didn't.

Mosango slowed to look behind him and Gneech and Satia caught up. "Let me down!" Septimus screamed. "I'll kill them all!"

"Keep going!" howled Gneech in return. "They'll kill us all!"

And on they went. Satia could feel the boots of the ogres shaking the floor with each stomp, their leader shouting orders that could be summed up as various ways to smash the companions into paste. They ran as fast as they could, until the wind of their passage finally swept the flame from Gneech's candle, plunging them into darkness. Although the ogres had torches, the way ahead was pitch black.

"What n—" Mosango started to ask, but the second word was abruptly cut off by an odd sort of descending cry, as though he suddenly started singing.

Before she could slow down, Satia felt Gneech tilting, his hand leaving her wrist as he scrabbled backward. "Satia!" the goblin cried, pitching down. "The floor! It's not there!" But it was too late, the jerk of his hand toppled Satia right into the pit with the others.

They fell, all kicking legs and flailing hands, bumping against the smooth sides of a glassy square. She fell more than twice the height of a man, Gneech right beside her, his staff smacking against her, the wall, himself, her again—really, anything he could reach—until with a *thump* they landed on top of Mosango and Septimus at the bottom of the trap chamber.

Disoriented by the fall, Satia rolled off the others and pressed her back against the wall of the pit. The chamber was slightly rectangular, as wide as the corridor above them but twice as deep and easily six feet long. She stood and reached up, but couldn't reach the top. Maybe she could with the tip of her sword if she held it up, but even then, the opening looked too far above. As she stared up forlornly, listening to the others scrambling to their feet, a torch jutted slowly out over the pit's aperture. It was followed cautiously by the confused face of one of the ogres, blackened and singed from the fire trap Satia had set off. One by one the other four clustered around the pit, staring down at them. "How we going to pound them, boss?" a burly one whispered out of the corner of his mouth.

The ogre in the sky blue armor rolled his eyes. "We don't have to pound anyone. They're stuck. We can decide what to do with them, or to leave them down there to die." He grinned broadly. This guy was clearly smarter than the average ogre.

"Zargut, if they die, that means the boy dies, and Thordane gets mad at us." As the second one pointed that out, his leader's wide smile faded. All right, then, he was only a *little* smarter than the average ogre.

The ogre leader's topknot hung down over his face as he knelt by the pit and stared in. "Gneech? Is that you?"

Everyone froze. Satia turned to stare at the goblin as Mosango stepped watchfully closer to Septimus. "You know the Ogre King personally?" she asked.

"What you want, Zargut?" Gneech didn't bother answering Satia. The goblin druid stood up to his full height, shaking his staff so that the trinkets tied to the crossbar jangled menacingly. "You better watch yourself or I'll magic you up but good!"

This drew a round of raucous laughter from the ogre thugs, but Zargut scowled. He waved them back and eyed Gneech warily. "You magic me, and our deal's off. You'll be hung out with the crows, side by side with your tribe." The goblin paled, and his hand fell, the staff shaking a bit in his grasp. Zargut continued. "You swore, Gneech, a promise I've kept. Maybe you were keeping it." Zargut stared at Septimus for a moment, then his dark eyes flicked back to Gneech. "Maybe not."

All eyes were stuck to the goblin. Gneech shifted uncomfortably, sneaking a look at Satia and Mosango. "So I make deal with Ogre King. So what?" He shrugged noncommittally.

Enraged, Mosango grabbed the goblin by the front of his robe and slammed him against the slick walls of the pit. "What did you promise him, you traitorous goblin?" He shook Gneech violently, rage brimming in his eyes.

Gneech cried out in pain. "I make promise long ago, before you walk with me, knight! Madman! Crazy human! Let Gneech go, or I will magic you until your arms . . . fall . . . off!" With each syllable, he kicked out at the knight until at last Mosango was forced to let him go or receive a particularly savage boot to his stomach. The knight stepped back, readying his weapon.

With an offended sniff, Gneech jerked his robes to settle back around his shoulders, standing up as tall as his hunched back would allow. "Ogre King and Gneech make deal long ago, about Irda treasure. I find treasure for Zargut, pay to free tribe."

"Hey . . . isn't that the same deal you made with us?" Satia began, but Gneech didn't give her time to build up steam.

"No, no . . . well, yes." Gneech shrugged. "But deal not same! You don't need treasure, you want treasure to find something to help Nox, yes? Zargut same. He not want treasure or steel." The goblin's eyes flashed up to the menacing ogres above them. "Not interested in treasure at all. Ogre want his keep back. To do that, must get sword. Ogre want Highlord of Dirt gone. He on our side!" Gneech brightened, waving his hands back and forth. "Right, Zargut?"

The ogre roared angrily down at them, his foul breath stinking up the whole pit. "You are a lying, cheating backstabber, Gneech!" Once again, Satia was impressed by the yellow-skinned ogre's vocabulary. Most ogres didn't know more than one word for any given thing, even for insults. This Zargut, clearly, was top of the class. "You're down here with the humans, stealing the treasure all for yourself. I trusted you, Gneech!" The ogre's hand tightened on the edge of the pit, and Satia swore she could hear the crack of his knuckles.

"Sword? Gneech, what sword?" Septimus looked the least offended of any of them, as if he'd fully expected to be betrayed. Knowing him and his mother, he probably did. "Is the sword useful?"

Gneech shrugged. "Is Irda sword. Keep sword. Will make Zargut officially king. When that happens, all ogres in the bog will come to him and fight for him. He will get rid of Highlord then!"

"And free your tribe?" Satia quirked an eyebrow.

"Yes. Well, after I pay him with money from hoard."

Satia bit her lip. Gneech was starting to sound like she did when someone caught her in a particularly poorly thought out lie. "Isn't that circular? You have to get the hoard so that you can help him take the keep, and then pay him with the hoard that you got so he could take the keep in the first place?"

"Maybe. Who cares? He get sword, become king, and my tribe goes free." Gneech shrugged, his shoulders sagging haplessly. "Zargut, you get us out of pit now? We go find sword for you?" he wheedled, smiling and showing toffee-colored teeth.

Zargut roared again, his face red and his knuckles white over the edge of the pit. Mosango and Satia shivered, and Gneech crouched behind the bits that dangled from his staff. Septimus just stared up at the ogre thoughtfully. Zargut snarled, "I think I should leave you all in that pit and pick your bones for the treasure when you've starved to twigs." Zargut looked them over, red faced. "But Thordane wants the boy."

"And you always give Thordane what he wants?"

Septimus asked, flicking a bit of the ogre's spittle off his tunic.

Zargut's brows clenched together. "I have little choice. The wizard has magic. He has a dragon. He has dragons and draconian allies. Most of my ogres fled into the bog. They do not think that an ogre can fight dragons or defeat wizards. That is why I want the sword of my forefathers, why I have struggled to be worthy of it. Because I still believe in the old ways, and I will restore them—and this keep. If I must be a slave to Thordane for now, if I must endure his ridiculous preening and pompous fluff, then I will, if that is what it will take to get the sword."

"And you're certain he will give it to you?" Satia raised an eyebrow.

"Why would he not?" Zargut's smile was bloodcurdling. "The sword wields its magic only in the hands of an ogre. It is useless to Thordane—though he does not know it is anything more than a worthless antique."

"And your soldiers?"

"They will see my power when I knock Thordane from his throne! Then they will look up into the sky and see once again the constellations of our forefathers, the glory of the ogres long ago. It will be a new beginning for our race, a new path to match our ancient glories." His unpleasant face shone with the thought.

Satia almost felt sorry for him. It was clear the four ogres standing up there with Zargut didn't understand what their leader was saying, nor did they care about "ancient glories." They'd probably be lucky if they thought beyond, "if we get them out of the pit, then we can smash them!"

"We don't want the sword, Zargut. We don't really even want the treasure," she began. "It would probably be worthless anyway. You and Gneech can have anything we find down there, but we've got to find a way to get Nox out. If getting you this sword gets you an ogre army—or whatever—then that's great by us." Mindful that the ogre's temper was short, Satia rushed on, "Especially if getting you that sword means that Nox and Septimus can get away from Thordane and take me home." She avoided any mention of Mosango's wild hopes, preferring to ignore their existence. The knight was completely mad—and Zargut would find out soon enough. No reason to rub it in.

The yellow ogre narrowed his eyes and rubbed his stubbly chin. "Why should I trust you?"

She couldn't think of any good reason, so Satia turned the tables. "Why should we trust you? You work for Thordane. You've already said you were ordered to take Septimus back to Thordane. And," she said, thinking quickly, "you're nothing but an ogre." She said the words with deliberate scorn. Gneech's eyes nearly bugged out of his head. "What do you know about honor anyway?"

Zargut stiffened. His ogre comrades, though they didn't really understand everything being said, read his movement as signal of an impending attack, and they raised their clubs threateningly. A strident growl from Zargut, and his men lowered the tree trunks they carried. "I understand how a human like you would have such a narrow viewpoint. We ogres have always known you were limited creatures. But if I were to give you my word on a deal, unlike this sniveling goblin, I assure you, I would keep it."

"But you won't do that," Satia managed to sound both suspicious and tempting. "You're not going to let us out of here. You won't take a risk on a bunch of humans just to get back your people's honor, your ancestor's sword, and Glorygate Keep. You're just an ogre, after all."

Offended, Zargut snarled so widely that Satia swore she could see his rear molars. Smacking aside one of the other ogre's clubs, Zargut lay on his belly and reached down his hand to grasp hers. "If you keep your word, little bug, I will keep mine. You and yours will come to no harm—but we will seek out the hoard right now. If we find my sword, then you will have earned my trust and friendship. If you fail, then I will crush your bodies, eat your bones, and deliver the little boy to Thordane on a steel platter. That is your choice." Instead of pulling her up over the side, Zargut jerked her close, until her nose was an inch from his and she was surrounded by his terrible breath. "Do we have a deal?"

"Y-yes," squeaked Satia.

Zargut grinned, and she could see every speck of rotted meat between his thumb-sized teeth. "Then let's get your friends out of that pit and go find my sword."

CHAPTER THIRTEEN

The lower portions of the keep twisted in on themselves like a vast ball of yarn with closed corridors, crumbled stone, and frustratingly clear floors through which they could see yet other passageways below. Occasionally, the floor was cracked, and they could ferry each other down with ropes. It was difficult, given that Zargut's girth—he was the widest of the five ogres—prevented them from going through anything but a good-sized hole.

Satia scouted—again—and tried to avoid traps—again—and occasionally triggered one, but fewer than before. She stopped only when they reached something impassable such as a stone wall, a crumbled bit of foundation sealing off the passage, or a tilting pit of shattered stone and knife-sharp glass shards leading down into impenetrable darkness—like the one in front of her now.

As Satia ran a hand through her hair, she burst

out, "We can't go any farther. Zargut and the ogres won't make it down that slope. They'll be chewed to bits on those shards. We have to go another way."

"No other way. This way leads toward center of keep. Other way blocked. Other other way head outside toward quarry. This is the way," Gneech said firmly.

"You're a Knight of Solamnia?" Zargut hovered over Mosango, staring down at the mad old man with disbelief. "The one who sold his armor?"

Mosango muttered grudgingly, "That was a long time ago."

"Hey, weren't you the one that—"

Mosango cut him off gruffly. "I'd rather not talk about it." The ogre laughed out loud at the knight's discomfort, but asked nothing more.

"We can't go this way. I don't even think there's a way out at the bottom of this pit. Even if there is, it'll probably be small—and just getting down there to check is dangerous. Trust me, those shards are *sharp*." Satia held out her finger for Gneech to see, bright blood welling from the tip.

The goblin knocked Satia's hand gently away. "Pfft. No matter. We go down."

Behind them, the other conversation continued. "You don't look like a knight." Zargut drew a deep, snuffling breath. "Don't smell like a knight." Ignoring everything with a supreme, self-contemplative look on his face, Septimus studied the wall with a sniff as the ogre and the human matched gazes.

Mosango grimaced. "I'm not a knight anymore."

"Once you take that kind of an oath, human"—the ogre loomed closer, his teeth gnashing—"you don't leave it behind."

Gneech started climbing carefully over the first jagged rocks, looking like a mouse climbing between a lion's teeth. "Rocks are sturdy. Pit is deep, but not too difficult to climb. Ogres will be fine! This is as far as I come before. Rocks block passage below. Big door. Gneech couldn't pull door free, but ogres can. I find some trinkets in rocks below." He stomped his staff on the uncertain ground and gestured at the waving items dangling from the crossbar. "So I think hoard must be just beyond door." He sniffed the air. "Can't tell if monster is still there . . . no smell other than dust and mold."

Satia leaned out over the edge, reaching out to run her hand along a jutting ledge of stone and glass. "You're sure the ogres can make it down there?" Her voice shuddered as she felt the tiny ridge of glassy blade along the edge.

The goblin smiled, wobbling on the stone, already

several feet down. He shrugged and grinned cockily. "What could go wrong?"

That was, of course, when the creatures attacked.

Lashing tentacles of articulated, rusted metal swung out from beneath the rocks, twisting like serpents around Gneech's legs and Satia's shoulders. Several chittering, oddly armored beasts rushed up from the shadows beneath several stones. They were covered in articulated plating, like armadillos, but four short, pawed, catlike legs scrambled underneath the arched body plates. Satia could see buglike eyes catching the light. In the back, each had a tail of the same whiplike, scaly rope as well, but tipped with sharp spikes in a circular pattern on the lumpy end.

Gneech screeched, his arms wrapped up in the tentacles coiled tightly around his body. They jerked the goblin down onto the rocks with a crash. Satia could see bloody scrapes on his arms where he was dragged across the glass and stone.

But she couldn't reach him. A tentacle latched onto her torso, pinning one of her arms to her side. It jerked as the creature reared up and pulled back, quickly lashing out with the other tentacle in the hopes of increasing its hold. Satia wrapped her other arm around a toothlike rock, not caring if the broken glass embedded in the granite cut her. The creature's tail smashed to one side, breaking stone and sending dust clattering down the side of the pit.

The third beast leaped far higher than Satia would have thought possible, and landed just behind her, facing the ogres, Septimus, and Mosango. It crouched, hissing, as its tentacles lashed and its barbed tail smashed the rocks. The creature stood about the height of a bear. One of the ogres fled immediately, another charged forward, and a third cast a searching gaze at Zargut as if to determine their leader's mood.

Septimus crouched, Mosango drew out the sword he carried, and Zargut bellowed. The first ogre to charge hit the armor-plated bug head on. The monster, moving as fast as lightning, crouched, wrapped its tentacles around the attacker's ankles, and hurled the ogre over its plated back. The ogre screamed as he sailed out into the air above the pit, arms and legs pedaling like a swimmer's. For a moment, he hovered there as the tentacles snapped free, then fell with a terrible crash into the black maw of the pit.

"I'm fine," whistled Gneech's voice from the pit when the horrible smashing finally hurtled to a stop. There was a momentary pause, and then Gneech added, "Ogre, maybe not so fine."

The last of Zargut's ogres swung his club at the

creature, but the armor-plated bug only hissed and lashed its tentacles from side to side, tearing into the ogre's face and arms. The ogre fell back, dropping his club over the side into the pit, and crumpled against the wall. The tentacles slashed wildly, ripping his clothes and tearing chunks out of his rough leather armor.

Mosango used the creature's preoccupation with the ogre to get close to their enemy. He brought the sword ringing down onto the monster's back, but it could not penetrate armored plates. Septimus ran blithely past the one in the hallway, unconcerned that it was killing one of the ogres. He threw himself on the rock where Satia hung, clawing his fingers into the tentacle. "Let go of her," he huffed, leaning in to bite the whiplike appendage. In the pit, the buglike monster shrieked.

"Help Gneech!" Satia yelled to Septimus, wriggling against the flailing tentacle that held her. She could no longer see the entire goblin in the pit, only his feet kicking out from behind one of the rocks.

"I want to help you!" Inexplicably, Septimus redoubled his efforts, fighting both the tentacle that held her and a second one that lashed viciously up at him.

Zargut reached out and slapped the hesitating ogre on the side of his head, triggering him from indecision.

"Save the goblin," Zargut commanded. "We need him to find the sword!" The ogre nodded and raced past the fight in the hallway, leaving Mosango and Zargut to handle the armored creature there. He ignored Satia and Septimus as well, even going so far as to climb over the flailing tentacles wrapped around each of them in order to stagger hastily down the side of the pit. Now *that* was dedication, Satia noted.

The sound of Mosango's sword ringing against the plating echoed with the labored huff of Zargut as he grasped the side of the beast. "Soft on the bottom, I'll bet." The ogre clamped his hands on the edges of the plating, eliciting a strange harmonic squeal from the creature, but in the narrow corridor—and with Mosango pounding it about the head and shoulders—the beast couldn't turn to prevent the leverage. With a heave and a strain of his gigantic muscles, Zargut began to lift the struggling beast. Tentacles swung about everywhere, whipping so wildly that they scraped fissures in the walls and tore Zargut's armor.

The creature's claws scrabbled for any purchase it could find against the glass and stone, but still Zargut lifted. The ogre let out a long, guttural yell as he toppled it to one side. It fell over with another shriek and a lot of tentacle flailing. The armor plating along its spine that had served so well to protect it now prevented it from rolling over, much like an upside-down turtle. The beast's paws slashed out, the claws as sharp as razors, and clattered against Zargut's chain mail. The ogre grunted with the force of the blow.

Septimus raised his head close to where Satia still struggled with the tentacle pinning her arm. He'd nearly bitten through the metallic tentacle—something Satia would have thought impossible. "Falling!" he gasped, the tentacle around his chest and waist choking out his breath. "Get ready!" Before she could argue, he pulled himself forward with a mighty effort and dug his fingers into the tentacle closest to the place he had been biting. Setting his feet against the rock, he jerked backward with all his power and arched into the tentacle's pull. The tentacle in his hands ripped apart, and the rock cracked from the strain. If he succeeded, they were both going to be—

SNAP! The tentacle between Septimus's fingers tore at the same time the rocky outcropping broke free of its moorings. The tentacle that held her arm tight to her side fell away in a snakelike clump, and the whole lot fell into the yawing darkness—rock, girl, dragon boy, and all. Satia's curly black hair caught in her mouth as she spun wildly out of control. She tried to shield herself from the landing by clutching her arms across her face. The fall ended with a massive thump and the crack of a rib as she landed hard against unyielding stone.

Groaning, Satia opened her eyes and looked up toward the light of the ogre torches at the surface of the pit. She could still hear Zargut and Mosango fighting their opponent, but there were far more immediate sounds closer by. Rolling onto her stomach, she pushed up onto her hands and knees to survey the scene. The ogre that had jumped into the pit to help Gneech had made it to the bottom. Although covered in cuts and torn fur clothing, he was standing on unsteady legs, tree-trunk club in hand. Gneech huddled at his feet, trying to regain his footing on the broken glass.

The creature that had been attacking Satia recoiled, mewling at an astonishingly high pitch as it lashed the stump of a bleeding tentacle. It still clutched Septimus in the other, keeping the boy's feet just far enough off the ground that he could gain no purchase. A second monster—the one that had been ready to chew up Gneech—perched on one of the jutting rocks nearby, tentacles flicking back and forth in readiness. One front paw, and part of the armor plating over that shoulder, was crushed as though it'd been caught in a giant vise. The ogre smashed his club against the wall with a threatening roar, and the creature flinched in response.

Gneech hissed and started chanting, twisting

his fingers in misaligned patterns of strange lore. His staff, which Gneech dropped when he was grabbed, lay beyond the creature, but even without the help of the staff's magic trinkets and charms, the goblin's fingers began to glow.

The ogre moved forward gingerly. Arching, the creature lashed out with one tentacle, but the ogre had frightened it, and the creature was tentative, too slow. The ogre caught the whipped tentacle in one thick-knuckled hand. With a flick of his wrist, he wrapped the squirming tentacle around his wrist and started to pull.

Drawing the knife from her boot and the sword from her belt, Satia faced the one holding Septimus. Her side hurt as if it were on fire, but there was no time to ask Gneech for one of his odd concoctions. Thinking quickly, Satia ducked low among the rocks. With a prayer, she hurled the dagger with all her strength, flipping it expertly in the air. Satia's jaw dropped as the dagger cut cleanly through the tentacle.

With a whump and a squeal of anger, Septimus fell to the floor. He jerked away the section of tentacle that was still wrapped around his waist and hurled it away with a snap of his jaw. The creature backed away, obviously hurt, both flailing tentacles chopped short. It yowled a strange, high-pitched noise and crouched down, sinking its claws into the rubble. Though injured, the monster wasn't giving up just yet.

There was a sudden explosion of light to the side, so bright that it seared Satia's eyes. She cried out, covering them, but not before she saw a blazing orb erupt from Gneech's outstretched hands and shoot toward the monster grappling with the ogre. It landed with another flash between the creature's tentacles, blinding the armored bug, who shrieked so sharply that the sound was almost out of hearing. The ogre seemed to be able to hear it, though, and he roared and jerked the creature forward the last few inches. The bug, frenzied and blind, reared back and scratched with its claws, digging them into the ogre's arm, but still he didn't let go.

The ogre punched forward with his club, but the beast wiggled and managed to turn sideways and grip the club in all four paws. The ogre tugged, but only managed to shake the creature back and forth. Gneech darted in behind him and started digging in the rocks where the creature ambushed them. He grabbed his lopsided staff with both hands and tugged on the shaky crossbar, making all the amulets dance. "Have to . . . get my . . . staff . . . free!" he gasped, letting go and digging again in the hopes of freeing the rag-wrapped stick from the grasp of heavy, fallen rocks.

When it finally popped free, the goblin laughed evilly and ran back to the trapped bug beast.

The ogre ignored Gneech. He tugged one way on the tentacle, then the other with his club, but the creature continued to hang between them, claws sinking into the club as it writhed blindly in the ogre's grasp. It was like some sort of confused taffy pull.

Gneech plucked one of the dangling trinkets free of the string that held it to his staff. He chanted and danced, taking short, quick steps on the rocky floor. He slipped on the glass a bit, but rolled forward, stubbornly determined to finish whatever he was trying to do. Finally he slammed his hand down on the beast's exposed belly. A trinket gleamed blue purple, and thick smoke hissed out between the druid's fingers. The bug screamed and writhed, but the ogre held it still. Gneech hummed and chirped happily, dancing in some primitive goblin ceremony as smoke poured out of his hand where it was pressed to the creature's flesh. After a moment, the monster went limp, and the ogre let go in surprise. It fell to the floor at his feet, the monster's entire belly eaten away as if by acid. "Gotcha," laughed Gneech victoriously.

Meanwhile, Satia and Septimus still fought the second bug in the pit. Although she couldn't see what was happening above them, it sounded as if Mosango and Zargut were having an even rougher time. She looked at Septimus, who frustratedly snarled, "Can't bite. Can't claw. No acid to breathe on it. I can't do anything!" His hands were bleeding from pounding on the creature's armored back. "Watch out!"

The monster's barbed tail lashed out, making Satia dance to the side to avoid the vicious spines.

"This is why humans use weapons." She tossed him the sword. "All you need to do is keep the thing's attention and stay in front of it—don't go near that tail!" Septimus hefted the sword, staring at it curiously, and Satia dug about on the ground to find the knife she'd hurled. They had only a few seconds before the creature worked up enough courage to charge them again. Picking up the sharp little blade, she grabbed his shoulder to keep his attention. "Keep it busy. I'll do the rest. And Septimus, as for saving me up on that rock?" She smiled lightly. "Thanks."

"Let's kill it," he responded simply.

Satia leaped from rock to rock, taking advantage of the fact that the creature's armor plating prevented it from looking directly above it. The monster had no tentacles left, so it was possible to approach, and Satia planned to get very close indeed. Septimus wove back and forth in front of it, turning the creature away. Although he had no clue how to use the weapon in his hands, it didn't matter—the steel sword wasn't going to cut through the creature's body armor plating anyway. He ducked around its sweeping tail with feral grace and banged on the monster's back. Well, Satia figured, that ought to keep it entertained.

Satia bounced above it, seeking an opening as it turned and twisted in an attempt to follow her swift form. When at last she had an opening, she took it. Darting quickly, she dropped onto the creature's back. It froze, stunned, and then let out another of its eerie, high-pitched shrills before it went wild, kicking and racing around with her on its back. Satia'd ridden a horse before. But this? This was something else entirely, even compared to riding a running horse. This was like being stuffed in a bag and slammed into a wall over and over again.

Gripping the ridge of an armored plate with her hand and clenching her legs around the monster as tightly as she could, Satia started digging at the plate with her dagger, slowly wedging the blade beneath it. Septimus leaped forward and blocked the swinging tail with the sword in a clanging ring, yelling fiercely. It worked. The bug charged forward instead of bucking, giving Satia a few more seconds to wiggle the knife deeper under the creature's armor. Part of the plate ripped away, and the monster squealed.

Septimus used the distraction to punch it in the face, just beneath the lip of the first heavy plate. It staggered as Satia raised the knife, and then she thrust it down into the gap between the plates with all of her strength. It sank in, biting deep into the creature's back, through the spine and down to where Satia imagined the heart might be.

The monster staggered again, weaving on its feet. Crossed knees and shaky ankles suddenly gave out, pitching the dead creature to the floor. Satia rolled to her feet, wincing as glassy shards cut her shoulders and arms. She stood up and shook the glassy shards out of her curly hair, tugging at each tight spiral until she was sure everything had come out.

"That was amazing, Satia." Septimus's eyes were wide. "The way you jumped on the boulders all the way onto its back!"

"No more difficult than jumping roofs in Gwynned," she said, suddenly shy. She tugged at her curls a little more, pulling them over her eyes.

"You're a good monkey." He reached out and patted her head as if complimenting a favored pet. Pausing to stare at him as if he'd gone mad, Satia fumed. He was never going to learn how to be . . . how to be . . .

Human.

From above them, the last sounds of desperate

combat echoed. "Mosango and Zargut!" she gasped, smacking her forehead. "I forgot about them!" Satia began to climb the glass and rock sides of the pit, not caring if her hands were cut or if the shards ripped the knees of her leather trousers. "Septimus! Push me up!" Septimus grabbed the back of her trousers and pushed, lifting her feet onto his shoulders. She struggled to climb up the rocks, but she was going too slow . . .

Until the ogre in the crevice with them grabbed her belt and lifted her above his head, hurling her completely up over the jutting, toothy rocks to the hallway passage above. Satia flew up with her arms pinwheeling in an attempt to get her balance. She crash landed in a heap somewhere in the upper passage. As she sat up, she realized that she had forgotten to take back her sword from Septimus.

Zargut had flipped the creature over, but in exchange, its claws had nearly torn through his chain mail. Mosango leaned against the wall, bleeding from a cut on his head where the tail had struck him. He still had his sword, but the creature's flailing paws had done such an effective job slicing Mosango every time he'd gotten close that the old knight didn't have a chance to use it. The monster now slid against the corner of the wall, using its tentacles and tail to push itself over. It lunged for Mosango, too fast for the knight's aged reflexes.

The creature nearly made it too, save for the fact that Zargut hurled himself onto the beast.

Ignoring the claws that dug into his flesh, the ogre pushed aside the beast's legs. "Kill it!" he roared, protecting Mosango so the knight could find an opening. Mosango pushed himself to his feet and lunged, sword sinking into the beast's heart. With a quiver, it fell still.

"You saved my life," Mosango breathed, stunned.

Satia tried to roll over onto her back so that she could get her legs beneath her. As she did, she heard Zargut yell for his ogres to report. The only one left to do so was the one that was still down the slope with Gneech and Septimus. Zargut sat down in the hallway, rubbing his arms and inspecting his wounds.

"You saved my life," Mosango said again. In a daze, he marched toward Zargut with his sword outstretched. Zargut realized the danger too late. Mosango's sword was in his face, the blade's point only inches from Zargut's eye. The ogre froze, face reddening in sudden rage.

"Mosango, no!" Satia screamed, rushing toward them.

The old knight's sword swished right past Zargut's ear, landing on the ogre's shoulder. Tapping once, twice, he passed the sword over the ogre's head and rapped Zargut's other shoulder with the blade. Mosango raised his sword before his face in a gesture of respect. "Rise, Sir Zargut, Knight of Glorygate Keep. I salute you."

CHAPTER FOURTEEN

argut, Satia, and Septimus—who had just managed to get over the lip of the slope in time to see this—stared baldly at the scene. Mosango snappily put away his sword in military style, thrusting it through the belt of his ragged clothing in a smooth, reflexive stroke. He offered his hand to the ogre to help the much larger warrior to his feet.

"The old boffer's gone completely mad." Septimus's voice echoed down the stunned hallway. "We're going to have to put him down."

"Septimus!" Satia shushed him. He wasn't helping.

Mosango tugged at the ogre, trying to help him up but really accomplishing nothing of use. Zargut placed his other hand against the wall and hefted himself up, regaining his feet with difficulty. "A knight?" The ogre's voice shook slightly, his eyes wide. His head tilted to the side and the odd topknot of hair fell down over one arm. "Is that . . . possible?"

The old man ignored the question, clasping the ogre's arm like a brother. "I'm afraid I have no sword to give you, Sir Zargut, as would be the tradition. All I can offer is my steadfast loyalty." It took a great effort for Mosango to stretch himself tall enough to kiss the ogre on both cheeks, but nobody was as stunned by it as Zargut. The ogre leaped back, shoving the knight away and scrubbing at his cheeks.

"What are you doing?" he spluttered. "What have you done?"

Before Mosango could answer, there was a shout from below, down the slope. "Here is door, hee hee!" Gneech sounded positively celebratory. "Blocks way to the treasure chamber! So thick, Gneech cannot move it alone. Here, ogre, move this aside. Lift that! No, no, *that!*"

Continuing with his demands, the goblin harassed the ogre below as behind them in the corridor, the ogre who had run away slunk back. He eyed Zargut to gauge his leader's temper. Lucky for him, Zargut was still stunned, watching Mosango the way someone might watch a snake. The ogre sniggered at the bemused expression on Zargut's face, only to be rewarded by a ferocious cuff to the side of his head that knocked him sprawling. Zargut grumped past him.

There was a horrible grinding noise below, followed by the sound of metal shrieking. Satia and Septimus ran to the edge of the slope and started carefully picking their way down. The knight—er, two knights—paused at the lip and waited to see what was below. As Satia and Septimus reached the bottom of the slope, they could see what Gneech was doing. There was a door against the wall of the broken-down area, as if there had been a hallway beneath the hall they were traveling down. The collapse of the mountain that had created the toothlike rocks and jutting glass had also opened a way into that lower area. The off-center door still leaned in its frame, blocking them from seeing what was beyond.

With a horrible clamor, the ogre pulled the massive iron door free. The top hinge ripped completely out of the wall and twisted on its lower edge in, leaving just enough room for a goblin to squeeze past. Gneech climbed over some nearby rocks, shimmied along the wall by the door, and pressed himself through the crack between the doorjamb and the frame. The ogre let go, and the door eased back a bit, but they could still see a bit of the goblin and his candlelight beyond the opening.

"What do you see?" Septimus called, cupping his hands over his mouth so the sound would carry. "Is it the treasure trove?"

"Hm." Gneech's voice floated back from farther down the blocked corridor. His voice rose questioningly in answer. "Yeeeeeeees?"

"Well, that doesn't sound good." Satia slumped against one of the rocks.

Zargut tromped down the rocky slope, his feet knocking free several of the rocks and causing a small avalanche all around him. His eyes flashed warningly. "Gneech, you lying rat fink! Do you see my sword?"

"Er . . ." the goblin called back, scuttling around inside the room beyond the door. "No."

Grasping the door in his massive fists as the other ogre redoubled his efforts, Zargut heaved the broken door. His strength was greater than that of his companion, and together they ripped the door free of its moorings. Beyond, Satia could see another hallway much like the one above, but this one's floor wasn't made of the strange glass that they'd seen before. Instead, it was covered in small, four-inch square tiles that were individually painted with ornate patterns. The walls, too, were painted, the once beautiful colors faded on the stone. Only the gold and silver paint remained in any quantity, glistening in thin coils along the wall.

A bit farther in was the main chamber. It was just as large as it had appeared from above, with arched walls and gracefully pointed ceilings of solid glass that faded up into darkness. The walls here were painted as well, faded colors and glittering metal strands along the smooth stone. Gneech was in the middle of the room, climbing over a pile of rotted tapestries and junked wooden furniture, cursing to himself. When the door fell away with an echoing clang, he froze like a startled raccoon.

Zargut stepped into the room, his eyes ranging over the piles of ancient trash. Where this room should have contained the bulk of the Irda treasure, it wasn't filled with steel, or weapons, or even gold, which Satia had heard used to be valuable in ancient times. Instead, every inch of the room held personal items: magnificent but shattered pottery, broken works of art, once-beautiful tapestries. A statue of a regal-looking person, big enough to be an ogre but far more refined and beautiful, stood at an angle in the center of the room. She had an arrogant look on her face, her hand held high in benediction or farewell, but now her body was spiderwebbed with cracks, one arm broken away, her graceful stone robe covered in moss. Slivered chunks of marble piled around the damaged floor at her feet.

Armor was stacked against the wall, no doubt once polished and clean, but now damaged, water-logged, and covered with rust and mold. Hundreds of years had turned it to rubble. Zargut lifted a piece, the steel breaking apart in rusty flakes under his fingers. He turned a ferocious gaze on Gneech, who started digging frantically through a pile of crumbling books whose pages were nothing more than mush. "It's here," Gneech muttered frantically. Zargut stomped across the room, and the goblin skittered over another pile of gilded but broken furniture. "Somewhere!"

"The sword!" Zargut reached for the goblin, red faced and steaming. "WHERE IS IT?"

"Somewhere! Maybe in outer room, under rock slide. Might have been another treasure chamber, they might have had it on display—"

"Under all the rocks?" Zargut bellowed. "Am I to get every ogre in the land down here to dig it up? The corridor would collapse! We'll never find it." The ogre wrapped his arms around the goblin, ready to squish him.

Mosango stepped up to the door and called out to him. "Ah, good Sir Zargut! Giving comfort to the goblin, are you? By Paladine, a truer knight than you has never been born." Satia stared at the old knight, and then looked to the ogre, who'd frozen stiff with shock just as he was lifting Gneech off the ground. The goblin kicked and squirmed in his arms, but the ogre turned his head slowly to stare at the madman.

Mosango crossed the room, hobbling on weak knees. "Poor Gneech. He came here looking for enough money to free his people, and there's nothing here that's valuable at all." Mosango bent down and let a handful of cracked stone from a once beautiful goblet fall through his fingers with a sigh.

"The goblin failed us! He lied to us! This is no treasure—this is trash!" Zargut's face was turning redder and redder, his knuckles whitening around Gneech's midsection. "I have no use for him other than as a stain on this floor."

Frowning, Mosango shook his head. "Those are not the words of a knight. You are better than that, Sir Zargut. Let us take the goblin and—" But whatever Mosango was about to propose, Zargut wasn't interested. The ogre responded with a massive roar, hurling the goblin away. Gneech flew through the air and landed in a heap near Satia. The girl ran to him, turning him over to see if the goblin still breathed.

"I am an ogre!" Zargut exploded, lifting his terrible club. He marched toward Mosango, and before the knight could respond, he tore the sword from the old man's belt and shoved him backward. With a snarl, Zargut placed the sword point on the floor and drove his foot down onto it in a mighty stomp, snapping it in two. "Not a knight!"

"You are whatever you choose to be," Mosango replied. He hunched over, pressing his hand against his chest to ease the pain from the ogre's shove. He looked the enraged Zargut in the eye. "Glorygate Keep fell, but you don't have to stay in the mud. What you want is to redeem this place. And that includes you. If you win this keep from Thordane, but you're as bad as he is, then what kind of victory is that? You're still living in the mud, Zargut. Still rolling around in filth with the rest of them."

"Stop it, Mosango!" Satia yelled as she chafed Gneech's wrists and tried to bring the goblin back to consciousness. "You're just making him angry!"

"He should be angry!" the withered old knight said. "He should be furious! Look at what he was! What the Irda—his ancestors—left him! And look what the ogres have done with it!" Mosango pointed a shaking hand at the statue of the beautiful woman, her features betraying a faint ogrish cast but her pose regal and her bearing stately. "They've fallen, like their keep, into dirt."

This only seemed to infuriate Zargut further. "You don't know me! You don't know my people!"

"But I do," Mosango corrected him wearily. "I've lived with the goblins for years. I've heard the legends of Glorygate Keep. I've seen your ogres bow before Thordane—and before him to others." There was no scorn in Mosango's weary tone, only sadness. Perhaps sensing that Zargut was unstable, Septimus stepped between Satia and Gneech and the ogre's large form. He'd dropped Satia's sword somewhere—she sighed—and was snarling like a wolf.

Zargut could barely contain his anger. He jabbed his finger in command to the ogre near Satia. "Tie up the boy. We're taking him to Thordane. Perhaps once the Highlord has him, Thordane will leave to fight his war—and we'll retake the keep that way."

"Zargut! No!" Satia screamed as the ogre grabbed Septimus before the boy could react. The two fought for a moment, but the smaller boy was quickly overcome. "You can't do this!"

"I gave Gneech a chance, trusted him. He failed. If it's the only chance I have to seize my keep, I'll do that—and worse," the ogre snarled viciously. Zargut turned to his henchman still lurking by the twisted door. "You. Bring the others. If they resist, kill them . . ."

"You can't do this, Zargut!" Mosango looked more hurt by the ogre's command than he had been by the vicious shove. "This isn't who you really are. Please, Sir Zargut. Show me your mettle." Mosango raised his hands beseechingly.

". . . painfully," Zargut finished, and stormed through the door.

Gneech looked up at Satia, obviously in pain. The wizened goblin touched his hand to his head, where he was bleeding. "Am I going to live?" he asked her half jokingly.

With a pinned-on smile, Satia put her arms under his shoulders and helped him stand. She tried not to notice how wobbly Gneech was, or how his eyes kept unfocusing. "Of course you are, Gneech," she replied easily. "We're going to get out of this somehow. I just know it."

It was the biggest lie she'd ever told.

CHAPTER FIFTEEN

The ogres took them through the keep to Thordane's great chamber despite Satia's pleas and Septimus's muttered threats. Gneech went along quietly, leaning on Satia. Mosango said nothing, resisted not at all. He shuffled along behind them, tugged forward by a length of rope tied to one ogre's belt.

Zargut shoved Septimus ahead of them through the gigantic, arched doorway. His ogres tugged the ropes on the others, not caring that Gneech still leaned on his twisted staff or that Mosango staggered with each sharp pull of the ropes. Satia looked at her companions, worry flooding her veins. They were all broken in one way or another, wounded inside and out. And who was she to save them? The only thing she could do well was . . . well . . . lie. Satia bit her lip.

The room was huge, the ceiling distant and half covered by darkness. There was a great hole on the far end, and small flying creatures she first assumed were birds, only to feel her heart drop through her stomach when she saw dragon wings—not feathery ones—carrying them upward. Draconians—the ones she'd seen earlier when she and Septimus had spied on the throne room. Satia gulped. She knew where she was. Ogres stood by the doorway, glaring down at her, and soon they were pulled in front of Thordane's throne covered in golden velvet. The rift in the ceiling had let the weather in, but the worst of the stains and rotting wood were at the far end of the hall. This area was as pristine as hard-working goblins could possibly make it.

Hisses of glee behind the dais and the flapping of cape-sized red wings drew Satia's attention. The two tiny dragons, Vex and Beset, curled around the back of the throne like massive, pony-sized dogs, their golden eyes twinkling in the torchlight. One snapped at his companion in barely restrained excitement, teeth flashing pale and white. The other clawed lightly at his twin in reproach. They fluttered a bit, then sat up, their wedge-shaped heads angling just above the back of the high throne to twist and stare directly at her. Satia gulped.

A man marched in from the far end of the room, golden cloak swirling around his ankles. His armor glinted—pure steel—with highlights of gold and black etched into the thick metal shoulders and the ridge of the solid breastplate. High boots stepped neatly over holes in the broken floor without losing the military beat of his internal drummer. Thordane. He turned his golden head toward them, hair falling neatly down over his forehead as his lips widened in a thin, self-congratulatory smile.

Zargut shoved her forward, pushing her to her knees before the throne. As Gneech lost her support under his arm, he fell too, his legs collapsing. Zargut shoved Mosango too, but the knight fell forward, missing his knees entirely to curl up on the floor before Satia. She could hear him muttering something that sounded like the Oath and the Measure of the Knights of Solamnia.

Septimus rumbled deep in his throat, tugging at the cord. "Mother!" he cried. Zargut backhanded him with a single blow that felled the boy instantly.

The sounds of people shuffling about must have awakened the dragon, or perhaps it was the red dragons speaking to one another in low whispers. Her eyes opened in slits, the golden color within glinting.

Septimus made a rumble deep in his throat, tugging at the cord. "Mother!" he cried. Zargut back-handed him with a single blow that felled the boy instantly. The sounds of people shuffling about must have awakened the dragon, or perhaps it was the red dragons speaking to one another in low whispers. Her eyes opened in slits, the golden color within glinting. The stone of the wall behind her seemed light by contrast, and Satia's eyes moved to it to give her some relief from staring into the darkness that was the dragon. There, along the back wall, Satia could see a dark metal hook implanted into the wall, fused magically into the stone. The chain that held the dragon.

Satia had wondered earlier how a chain, even such a massive one, could hold a dragon like this in place, but now up close, she could see that this was no ordinary chain. There had to be something magical about it to hold the massive dragon in the room—which seemed a mighty magic, indeed, to Satia.

"Septimus?" The dragon's voice was a whisper, but it came with an overwhelming, earth-shattering rush of dragonfear. Obviously, the collar didn't stop her from simply being terrifying, though Satia figured from Thordane's taunts earlier that it had some kind of effect on Nox's ability to cast spells. The fear swept over them all like a great wind. Gneech writhed and squirmed on the floor, whimpering. Even Satia couldn't suppress the squeal that tore from her throat, but Septimus pushed himself to his feet as though he felt nothing at all.

"Hi, Mother."

The dragon leaped forward, her body shifting as gracefully as a cat's. Nox stretched herself the full length of the chain, tugging so hard that the collar bit into the scales at the ruff of her neck and drew a faint trail of dark blood. Her nostrils flared, sniffing at the boy standing at the base of the dais. Golden eyes snapped open, feral and sharp, taking in every detail. "My son."

The two red dragons curled by the throne snarled and bristled, their eyes narrowing and the red flanges behind their horns spreading in an attempt to appear more frightening. Septimus dismissed them without a word, taking another step toward his mother, but Satia could see that her companion's hands were clenched into sweaty fists. The dragons might be small—but Septimus was *human*.

"He is well, you'll see."

Satia had been so overcome by dragonfear that she hadn't seen Thordane climb the dais, hadn't noticed him recline into the throne with the attitude of a conquering emperor. "He will continue to be so, as long as you obey me."

Satia could feel Mosango kneeling beside her, the rope that bound her hands connected to his. He stared at Nox, eyes wide, face pale. Satia could see his fingers twitching as if aching to hold a sword, and the crazy old man's beard almost curled with trembling realization.

"By Paladine," she whispered. "Hold it together, Mosango. They'll kill you if you try anything."

"Black . . . dragons . . . children of Takhisis . . . my *enemies* . . ." Mosango was quietly raving, spittle flying out with each bitter word.

"He didn't tell you." Although Satia had known, she hadn't expected this reaction. Mosango was practically crumbling from the inside. "I'm sorry, Mosango."

"You knew?" Mosango didn't take his eyes off Nox. "You knew he was . . . one of them? And you worked with him?"

"It's not like that . . ."

"This is more a 'little' lie, Satia. Black dragons are evil. They fought against us in the war. My friends were killed by dragons like these. My squire . . ." Mosango gulped. "He died because of them."

"What happened to him, Mosango?" She needed to keep Mosango talking, keep him interacting with her until he regained his composure.

"My squire wanted to fight the dragons. The war was almost over. There were few battles left. We had won. But Loris wanted to fight on dragonback, just once." Mosango's face was stricken. "I let him go. I dressed him in my magic-reinforced armor, thinking it would protect him. I told him how to mount my dragon. And I watched him go into the dawn with the others—for the last battle."

"He didn't survive, did he?" Satia guessed.

It seemed to take Mosango an eternity to answer. "They brought his body back on his shield. Everyone in the order of knights knew I'd allowed it. I let Loris go in my place, and he died." Mosango glanced up at the armor Thordane was wearing, shivering as if carrying a burden of ice. "It was my fault. I killed him. I should have been in the battle that day against dragons like these . . . I should have been the one to come back in that armor. Loris . . . Loris, I'm sorry. I can still see them flying out, sun on silver wings, sun on bronze wings . . ." Mosango shook, falling silent with pain.

Gneech crawled closer to them, his flat eyes reflecting the torchlight. "What's with him?"

"The dragonfear's overcoming him," she lied quickly. "He's trapped in a bad memory." Thordane and Nox were still eyeing one another, looking for some weakness in the other's resolve, but the ogres were focused on the three prisoners huddling at the base of the dais. "We've got to get him out of it before he does something dangerous."

Gneech had managed to keep his staff by leaning

on it, using his wounds to justify the possession of the tattered, rag-covered length. Now he used it to thump Mosango about the head and shoulders. Mosango groaned, shaking his head. He muttered his dead squire's name softly and fell silent again.

Frightened that their squabbling was going to draw too much attention, Satia looked up at the dais where the red dragons had crept forward, smelling the air as if testing the limits of their own patience. Satia had seen that look before—it was the same one Septimus wore when he swept her off that roof in Gwynned. *They were hungry.*

Thordane had risen from his throne languidly. He walked across the dais, pausing when he stood beside Septimus, and placed his hand on the black-haired boy's shoulder. "You *will* serve me, Nox," he said, making Satia wonder what she'd missed of the conversation. "I swear it." Thordane's other hand flashed out from beneath his long cloak. Gripped against his palm was a long dagger, wickedly curved like a sickle. He brought it up to Septimus's shoulder in a single, fluid gesture.

"Your puny blade can't hurt my son," Nox laughed, the air rippling with her disdain. "He is a dragon."

"Not anymore." Thordane gritted a smile in return. "Thanks to your spell, he's human. And humans can be cut very easily." As if to show his point, Thordane dug the edge of the knife into Septimus's shoulder, ripping through the black tunic and into the skin. He turned the weapon on its point, keeping the curve of the knife close to the boy's neck. Septimus cried out, but something held him still. Apparently Thordane had cast a spell to freeze his muscles as stiff as a board.

Keeping the knife close, Thordane lifted the boy's arm and Satia realized what was making Septimus stand so quietly. Thordane had fastened a cuff made of the same iridescent metal as the collar on Nox's black-scaled neck onto Septimus's left wrist.

"You cast a spell on him, remember? He's not human by his own will, so he's not protected by the magic of a true dragon. I doubt he'll be able to fight the bracer's power even half as well as you fight your collar. He's genuinely nothing but a small, helpless boy. My slave." Thordane shoved Septimus forward toward the throne. "Kneel." The single word was delivered with a wealth of hate and satisfaction.

Septimus fought against it, his hands clenching, his body writhing. Finally, with a choking sob, his knees collapsed, dumping him to the floor before Thordane. Satia could see tears streaming down Septimus's cheeks.

Nox howled in anguish, lashing out against her

collar, and her cries overwhelmed the muted sniggers of Vex and Beset. The great black dragon's claws swiped at the air near the dais, too far away to threaten the mage or his little dragons. Her trumpet echoed from the walls of the keep, shaking it to its foundations, but she could not reach Thordane.

Smirking, Thordane settled once more into his throne, raising one booted foot to prod the unmoving Septimus. Reveling in Nox's obvious rage, Thordane continued. "He can only do as I command. Were he a dragon again, I'm certain he would fight me. But sadly, only you can undo that spell. And you cannot do so with the enchanted collar around your neck. I must thank you, Nox, for providing me this perfect opportunity to ensure your obedience."

Nox snapped her head on the end of her elegant neck, roaring up at the ceiling in frustration. "You cannot hold him forever!"

"On the contrary, Nox. I think you'll find otherwise," Thordane practically purred. "He's mine now, Nox. As are you." One of the red dragons—Vex, Satia thought—rubbed his barrel-sized head against Thordane's leg. "You now serve me."

For the first time, Satia could see an emotion on the tremendous dragon's muzzled face that was neither rage nor disdain. Her golden eyes—two sorrowing, shining pools—stared down as her neck arched and curved. Very gently, Nox lowered herself to within a few feet of Thordane and her son, her nostrils flaring as she drew in a deep, shuddering breath. She opened her mouth, fanged white teeth glinting, gossamer threads of acid dripping down between them, and sighed out a long, whispering moan. "Let him go, Thordane. Let him go, and I will serve you." The words clearly cost the dragon, and her wings twitched with the effort.

"You know, Nox, I *almost* believe you. If I didn't know full well that you were Takhisis's spawn, I might even let him go." Thordane grabbed Septimus's jet black hair, staring into the boy's eyes with malicious glee. "But I think, instead, I'm going to—"

Whatever Thordane was going to do to Septimus, Satia never found out. Before the wizard could finish the sentence, Mosango leaped to his feet and screamed. It shocked them all. Even the dragon jerked her serpentine head back in surprise. The sound rocked through the chamber, startling the ogres that were supposed to be guarding them. Mosango snatched away Gneech's staff and held it up by the short end, hands pressed against the tilted crossbar as if the staff were a greatsword. Rags swung everywhere and the little trinkets that were hanging from the crossbar fluttered all around Mosango's arms.

"Hear me, dragon!" Mosango held aloft the unwieldy weapon and spoke as though he were leading armies instead of standing in mud-covered rags. "You will not harm that boy!"

Then, Mosango charged.

CHAPTER SIXTEEN

osango ran toward the dais, his frail legs carrying him in fits and spurts of rage. He stumbled once, his hand pressed to the floor as he lunged ahead, refusing to stop even when the ogres roared and pulled out their clubs. The old Solamnic Knight moved like a trained warrior, but his stiff joints belied the image of the shining hero come to rescue them all from harm. Vex and Beset spread their wings, snarling, and one lashed forward to snap at the air just in front of the old knight. Mosango tripped past them, not even noticing their efforts. His eyes were fixed on the black dragon at the end of the room.

"Stop! Mosango!" Satia reached for him, but he slipped from her grasp in an instant, the fluttering, rag-covered staff held high. His eyes were fixed on Thordane and Septimus as if they were the only two living things in the massive chamber. Gneech jerked back on Satia's frozen arm before the ogres rushed past them, huddling close to protect her.

Thordane, who was concentrating on the dragon and the boy in his hands, was taken completely by surprise. It took the wizard a fraction of a second to realize the danger. By then, it was too late. Mosango brought the ragged staff down on Thordane's shoulder with a shockingly loud clang.

Clang? Satia thought. But the staff isn't made of . . .

Thordane's shoulder dropped, the knife falling from his shaken hand. Septimus didn't move or flinch, his body still controlled by the magical bracer clamped to his forearm. Thordane, on the other hand, fell back a step, snarling as the old knight raised his ungainly weapon above his head. "Have at thee, scum!" Mosango howled madly, swinging Gneech's staff around his head in an oddly valorous gesture that seemed to confuse Thordane even more. Rags were swinging everywhere, some falling from the length of the staff, others tearing and fluttering like banners in the path of Mosango's broad sweep. Beneath the rags and tangling threads of trinkets, something glinted.

"Gneech!" Satia grabbed the goblin's shoulders and shook him lightly. "Where did you get your staff?"

"In the pit where the monsters were, first time

there," Gneech snapped, scrabbling to get away. The ogres closed in on Mosango. "We have to stop them," the goblin said bravely. "I'll start. You finish."

"What?"

But it was too late. Gneech was already chanting. He waggled his fingers and started jumping in a circle, screeching at the top of his voice. Clearly, this was going to be one whopper of a spell. One of the three ogres paused, turning back with a thickly quizzical glare. With nowhere to hide, Satia palmed the dagger from her boot again and got ready for a hopeless fight. "C'mon, you!" she yelled at the ogre. "I've killed ten times your like, and chopped them up for shoe leather! Do you really think I'd be afraid of a little guy like you?" The ogre stared at her, stunned by her boldness. Well, at least she could still lie.

"Fool!" Thordane spat, brushing a tatter of rags from his steel-armored shoulder. The ebony and gold inlays glittered in the light, and his golden cloak swirled around his ankles. "Do you dare challenge me?" He thrust Septimus forward into Mosango's hands, forcing the knight to catch the boy.

Thordane laughed, pointing a steely finger toward Mosango. "Nox, Septimus." He swept his arm to encompass Mosango, Gneech, and Satia too, and smiled. "Kill them all."

Septimus turned in Mosango's arms, clutching at the knight's ragged clothing. With a vicious claw of his hand, he tore at the knight's throat, leaving long, bloody scratches across Mosango's collarbone and chest. Mosango stared down at the boy as though he'd turned into a pillar of fire right in his arms. "Loris?" the knight asked weakly, the weapon tumbling from his hand. He spoke his squire's name again, trying to understand what was going on.

"My name's not Loris," Septimus snarled through clenched teeth. "I'm a dragon! I'm not your squire! I'm not even your friend!" Tears ran down the boy's pale cheeks as he swiped again at the knight, but this time the stroke lacked conviction. Still, the magic of the bracer forced Septimus to keep fighting. Mosango batted at the boy's arms and fumbled backward, unable to bring himself to harm Septimus.

"Get the girl and the goblin!" Zargut ordered, following Thordane's command. "Leave the old knight to the dragons." The three ogres in the room obeyed, circling toward the crouching Satia and the chanting, dancing Gneech. Despite her brashness, which had slowed the ogre advance for a while, they were far more afraid of their leader than of a girl—and Satia knew it.

But even as the three ogres charged and swung

their clubs, Satia's eye fell on a bundle of rags lying at Mosango's feet. The last layer of rags had fallen away from Gneech's staff. Now it gleamed in the light, steel shining under layers of grit. "The sword of the Ogre King!" Satia froze in her tracks. Blinking, she spun on one heel and pointed at Zargut. "The sword!" she yelled. "It's right there in front of you! Don't you see? Gneech's staff!"

Zargut's brow furrowed and the other ogres slowed, sensing his uncertainty. Zargut took three long steps forward. He slowly turned his gaze to the length of steel lying at Mosango's feet. Though the crossbar was still crooked and the bronze wiring on the hilt had long ago turned green, the edge gleamed in the torchlight.

Zargut hesitantly leaned forward and touched the sword on the floor. He pulled away the ragged scraps that clung to it, straightened the loose crossbar, and clamped the hilt firmly in his hand. The sword was long and thin, its blade no thicker than its hilt, the crossbar a mere ornament at the low end of the sword. Zargut held the weapon up before his face, so close that his breath misted the steel. "The sword of my forefathers," he whispered. "At last."

"Kill them!" Thordane yelled again, his voice carrying with anger. There was a sound of sucking breath and flapping leather, the echo of claw on stone. Satia jerked her head around to see what was happening. Nox had moved to place both legs on the dais, leaning in to reach out toward her son. The dragon's wings were outstretched like a billowing black cloak, her whip-like tail lashing back and forth. The scar that wove up Nox's legs was a bloody marker, shining in relief against the darkness of her skin, and the ruff that had lain flat now stretched upward in a stiff, angry fin. She roared, and the metal collar tugged at the end of her chain. Nox was strong, stronger than Septimus and able to resist the collar's mental command. But her eyes landed on her son, and she roared again, a hint of rebelliousness edging the ferocious tone.

Of course, Satia thought to herself, it wasn't that the dragon wouldn't have killed them all anyway—Septimus had been bringing her home to eat her, after all—but rather that she hated to do it this way, enslaved. Nevertheless, Nox lashed her head forward, and Satia felt the crushing weight of dragonfear pushing her to the ground.

From the far end of the chamber, where the ceiling had broken away, there was a resounding answer. A flight of draconians, their orangey, scaled skin catching the last rays of sunlight coming through the hole, dived toward them with swords drawn. Some carried two weapons and others hid the edge of their blades behind round shields of leather and wood, but all of them responded to Thordane's call with eager intent. They faced a dozen draconians, four ogres, Septimus gone crazy, and Nox. And to top it all off, the wizard and his red dragons hadn't even moved from the dais. They were definitely in trouble.

"Sir Zargut!" Mosango's voice rose above the din. "It is time to show your quality!" The ogre lifted his eyes from his sword, mouth opening in protest, but Mosango would have none of it. "Knight and brother, I call upon your honor to aid us in freeing your keep and your people!"

"Ridiculous," spat Thordane. "Ogres can't be knights. They're idiots with no sense of honor. Zargut's place is kneeling before my boot, along with the rest of his people."

Something snapped in the ogre's eyes. Uncaring, he roared a challenge in the ogre language, his green tail of hair snapping about in the wind of Nox's wings. The big ogre lifted his sword in expert hands and leveled the blade at Thordane. "If you love your freedom, boys," Zargut commanded his soldiers, "attack!" Beyond him, Satia could see Mosango's face shining with joy despite the bloody gashes from Septimus's fingernails.

Just then, Gneech finished his spell. He lifted

gnarled hands to the ceiling, shrieking a high-pitched, howling cry that shivered the wooden railings of the ceiling. A golden light shimmered around the goblin's hands, arcing from his fingers to surround his body. The light spread to Satia and Mosango, and then on to the ogres, wrapping them all in shimmering gold. The dragonfear lifted, and Satia could breathe again. Her arms seemed to move faster, she regained her footing in a snap of motion, and her dagger felt almost infinitely light in her hand. She let out a surprised laugh, amazed at the spell's facility. Gneech laughed maniacally in return and started chanting again, jumping up and down and flapping his arms like a chicken. "Finish it!" he panted between cavorting leaps as the draconians swept in to attack.

They came in a wave, wings outspread and swords lowered. Two of them plunged to crouch at Thordane's feet, ready to defend him against any attacker. Four more landed within reach of Zargut, and three around Septimus and Mosango, though they seemed momentarily content to see what the boy would make of the old knight. One swept just over Satia's head, its sword sweeping close enough to cut off a few of her curls. The others plunged into Zargut's ogres, swords chipping into solid oak clubs.

Nox opened her mouth, her throat moving

convulsively as she tilted her head to the side. From between her long white teeth, a jet of sticky acid flew out. The long stream of greenish gray sickness splattered across the floor where the ogres were fighting Thordane's soldiers. One of the ogres howled in agony, his body steaming. The acid etched away the wood in deep scores where it landed on his club, and dissolved the leather and chain like soft paper before water where it had struck his armor. Satia averted her eyes before she could see what it did to his skin. The ogre screamed once more, and then fell to the floor, silent.

However, Nox's shot hadn't been targeted just at the ogre. Satia could see one of the draconians that had been fighting the ogre fall to the ground beside him, writhing in agony. Acid had burned its wings to tatters, and one arm withered against its side, its armor crumbling as well. After only a second, the draconian's body stiffened, its skin hardening into gray stone. It seemed that the dragon was forced to obey Thordane, but she could still be spiteful.

Enraged, Thordane pointed at the combat, snarling something low and vicious. Vex and Beset sprang to their feet in joyful bounds, slinking forward with wings outstretched and eyes aglow. Beset started chomping on the air, clearly trying to work up flame in his immature bellows. Vex, the smaller of the two, scraped the ground with iron-colored claws and flapped his wings viciously, preparing to take to the air. This was real trouble, Satia thought.

"Satia!" Mosango yelled. "Get Septimus! I must fight beside my brother!"

With no choice but to abandon Gneech and hope for the best, Satia ran toward Mosango and dived onto Septimus. Her body hit the boy's with full force, sending them both reeling across the floor. Before she could even get her bearings, Mosango was away. Zargut pulled Satia's short sword—the one she had seized in the depths from the hobgoblin—out of his belt, pitching it across the room to Mosango's eager hand. With it in his grasp, the old knight paused to salute Satia and Septimus. "In your honor, m'lady, and for my squire's good name," he pledged. "This evil will be overcome."

"I'm not your squire!" Septimus struggled to get out of Satia's grasp, clawing her arms where she held him. "Mother! Help me!" Satia gulped, looking up as Nox's gigantic, wedge-shaped head rotated to orient on her. Uh-oh.

Flame rushed past Satia's body, heating her with its wake. Beset cried aloud to see it miss, and started churning air again, crouching to gulp down great breaths in preparation for another gout. From the air, Vex swooped down toward Satia, and she was forced to shove Septimus down, dropping to her face on the floor in order to skid beneath those gnashing claws. Vex screeched in disappointment, wings flapping in an ungainly attempt to rise into the air again.

"Let me go!" Septimus swung at her, and Satia absorbed the blow, grunting.

"No! If I do, you'll hurt someone!"

"Dirty human!"

"You're one to talk," she replied, returning his punch with one of her own, straight to his chin. It connected with a snap, and the two of them rolled across the floor through the pandemonium.

Mosango and Zargut fought side by side, two more ogres flanking them. The two battled against an overwhelming amount of draconians, swords ringing against one another in tight combat. Mosango was slow, but his knowledge of combat was greater than that of the draconians, who had apparently fought only things that feared them. A single blow from the clubs of Zargut's ogres was enough to crunch bone, and the sword of the Ogre King sliced through his enemies like a knife through butter. Before Satia knew it, four of the draconians had turned into statues, crumbling to the floor in piles of dust.

Thordane took half a step backward on the dais, raising his hands to cast a spell. *"Atah par nibami!"*

Suddenly, the floor all around Satia started shaking. Small explosions of force welled up beneath the stone and wood of the chamber floor in a row of percussions, bursting beneath the feet of Zargut, Mosango, and the draconians around them. The draconians simply leaped into the air, wings spreading to carry them above the danger, but the ogres and the old knight had no such ability. The detonations all around them hurled stone and wood into their eyes. The debris pounded against their armor and sliced into arms quickly raised to shield their faces.

The airborne draconians prevented Vex from swooping again, and Satia scrambled to her feet despite Septimus continuing to wrestle against her grasp. Beset warbled from the dais, encouraging Vex to try again. He loped down from the raised plateau of stone and sent his next burst of flame upward, scattering the draconians—at least, those who didn't become engulfed in fire and fall screaming to the floor of the chamber. Beset beamed up at Vex, eyes sparkling and something like a draconic grin curling his lips back over his teeth.

Not all dragons, thought Satia, were blessed with brains.

But Thordane wasn't the only spellcaster here. With a panicked shout, Gneech completed his crazy dancing. He punched out with one fist at the end of his cavorting, and a brown fist of stone formed over his fingers. Gneech flexed once, then spun and lashed out toward Thordane. *"Gerzhunt!"* The stone fist flew off Gneech's hand, propelled by the power of magic. As soon as the fist was in the air, it swelled to the size of a small dog and whizzed past Satia and Septimus with a shriek. The two draconians guarding Thordane spread their wings and tried to leap out of its way, but they were too slow. The giant stone fist plowed into them, knocking them backward into the wizard. All three toppled back against the wall behind the throne. The rocky wall cracked from the force of the blow, splintering in a spiderweb pattern, and bits of stone rained down from the roof above. Vex bugled a laugh, and Beset chortled on the dais.

In between her struggles to hold Septimus back, Satia could have sworn she saw Nox smile.

Thordane chanted for a moment, then, with a mighty burst of strength, rolled the boulder off his legs. His magical armor had shielded him from the worst of the blow's damage, but not so the draconians, who had turned to stone at their deaths. His face pale with anger, he wiped their dust callously from his breastplate. He ripped away his golden cloak, leaving it pinned beneath the heavy stone fist, and pushed his way to stand beside Nox's leg.

One of the other ogres fighting with Mosango and Zargut had fallen beneath the weapons of the draconians, but the knight and the Ogre King still stood back to back, swords weaving in elegant harmony. The old knight fought with all the courage of his past, urging the ogres on to greater feats of strength against their foes.

Vex swooped again, and this time Satia was forced to loosen her grip on Septimus in order to dodge aside. Free at last, Septimus rolled over to sit on her, batting away the dagger she jabbed halfheartedly at him. "I'm going to tear you apart," he said, tears pouring down his face. "Stupid human! You're beneath me! You're nothing but a worm!" But his fingernails barely cut her, and although he punched her in the stomach, the blow hardly stung. "I'll kill you!"

"Septimus! Look! Your mother's choking on an ogre!" Satia pointed toward the dais. Despite himself, the black-haired boy spun, glancing with fear toward the big dragon. In his hesitation, Satia seized her chance. Instead of stabbing him, she dropped the dagger and grabbed his forearm with both hands, tugging at the bracer. It came away in her hands, leaving Septimus free.

"Liar," he breathed. His eyes widened as he realized what she'd done.

Satia shrugged and flashed him a grin. "You better believe it."

CHAPTER SEVENTEEN

Thordane gestured, and lumps of sticky fire rained from the ceiling, pouring down as though someone had upended a gigantic lit candle. Vex yelped and swung aside, his wings beating in frustration and fury as he was unable to reach his prey. The two draconians left of the phalanx flapped their wings and soared quickly over to their master, realizing that the fight had suddenly shifted balance. The ogres and Mosango were not so lucky. Fire scorched their skin, blackened their armor, and even clung to the Ogre King's sword as he lunged after the fleeing draconians. Beneath the searing rain, Mosango fell.

Zargut roared in anger and kneeled beside his friend. In answer to Satia's stare, he said, "He will live— but only if we get him assistance for his wounds."

"Gneech!" Satia began, but the goblin was already on his way.

He crawled over the bodies of the fallen to

Mosango's side. Huddling beneath a tilted shield so that the last drops of fiery rain would not harm him, Gneech reached up and jerked down a few talismans still hanging from the crossbar of Zargut's sword. "So, that was the sword, eh?" he grunted. "Looked like a piece of trash to me." The goblin began tending to Mosango, but fear crossed his flat, brutish features. He shook his head once, and then bowed over his work.

Vex swooped to land back on the dais, grumpy and enraged, and hissed at Beset when the other dragon attempted to comfort his twin. "Surrender now!" Thordane's voice rumbled through the chamber like thunder, augmented by his powerful magic. The little red dragons bugled in exclamation, eager to see their master's will executed. Satia looked around at her friends: Zargut stood over Mosango, sword raised but all of his soldiers fallen. Gneech was too busy saving Mosango's life to prepare a magical attack, and Septimus . . .

"Septimus, I've got a plan. Take me up there. Take me to Thordane." She said the words very quietly, still pinned under the boy's grasp. He narrowed his eyes and clenched his fists against her shoulders. Without appearing to move, Satia managed to tug the sleeve of Septimus's left arm down, covering the bare skin where the bracer had been.

Kicking off of her, Septimus twined one hand

into her hair and grabbed the neck of her shirt with the other, twisting Satia around before him. Letting go of her hair, he pulled her arm up behind her back and forced her to rise with him. Satia was the very image of a struggling prisoner. She was pretty sure that the bruises and cuts he'd given her while they were fighting on the ground completed the sight. Zargut choked back a howl of fury, ready to charge across the hall and chop Septimus in half, but a covert glance from Satia stopped him in his tracks.

"Smart girl," Thordane purred, stepping forward to mount his throne again. "You see, Zargut? She understands her position all too well. Put your sword down, betrayer, and I'll deal with you in a moment. If you so much as flinch right now, this girl dies at the hands of the dragon boy."

Half convinced by Thordane's words, half trusting Satia's hidden wink, Zargut obeyed. He lowered the tip of the sword, pushing against the stone draconians that ringed the area he and Mosango had made their stand. Zargut's eyes smoldered, and his hands clenched into yellowy fists on the hilt. He ground his teeth so loudly that Satia could hear it as she took her first step up onto the throne's platform.

Nox loomed over the throne, her feet placed at the edge of the dais, her chain stretched to its fullest.

Satia saw that if Nox stretched out her neck she could almost reach the throne and the man reclining in it—but not quite. The dragon's golden eyes took in every detail of her son and his captive, and she flared her nostrils where she saw that Satia's blows had bruised the boy. Unashamed hatred and rage made the dragon shiver in her tracks, her black tail lashing back and forth with a crash against the stone walls. Dragonfear washed over Satia once more, but Gneech's odd golden shield still held, protecting Satia against it. Nevertheless, she felt it was only right to cower a bit and moan.

The two red dragons weren't paying Nox any attention, their eyes riveted on Satia and Septimus. Beset's tail flicked restlessly, and Vex licked his lips, no doubt hoping to be allowed the first bite. Satia gulped and started to rethink her plan. But no. It was this—or nothing.

Septimus wrestled Satia across the dais, shoving her forward until she stood between the two draconians, directly before the throne. She could see Nox leaning into her chain, the hook in the wall shivering with the weight of her body. The iridescent collar that prevented the dragon from using her magic shimmered about her neck as the bracer had on Septimus's arm. Thordane only smiled.

He reached out to lift Satia's chin, turning her head from side to side. "Pretty. A bit young, but she will make a fine slave. Your name, girl?"

"Satia." She jerked away from his touch. "My father is prince of Gwynned. If you harm me, he'll raise an army to rip you from your little keep and destroy you."

Taken aback by her ferocity, Thordane choked out a bark of laughter. "An army? Against my dragons! Your father must be powerful indeed!"

"More powerful than you know." Pulling on the stories Mosango had told them, she pushed on. "He fought with the Knights of Solamnia in the War of the Lance. He rode a copper dragon. That dragon still lives, and it's his friend." She couldn't help an involuntary glance up at the huge black monster hovering over them, just out of reach. "If you dare fly your filthy black dragons into his territory, he'll cut you down like chaff." Her legs were shaking so hard that Septimus was holding her up with his fake prisoner act, but she kept her body stiff and proud. "He killed many Highlords during the war. He fought against the flying citadel too." She stopped there, afraid that she might have gone too far. The red dragons hissed at Thordane's side, suddenly uncertain.

Thordane pondered this, lifting a hand to stroke

Vex's forehead thoughtfully. As he looked away, Satia managed to catch Zargut's eye, nodding toward the side of the dais. Behind her back, she made a little pointing gesture to one side. Could Zargut tell what she was pointing at? Would he understand?

Thordane stiffened and turned to stare at her, and she couldn't look back to see if Zargut was moving. The ogre seemed more intelligent than the rest of his kind. Now he was going to have to prove it.

Thordane spoke eagerly, his ire raised by Satia's story. "I think I remember your father. Tall man with a long blue banner . . . some sort of symbol on it. He wasn't a knight, but he fought with them. Yes, I remember him." Taken in by her lies, Thordane pressed her. "He's not a wizard? He has no magic?"

"He may not have spells, but he doesn't need them." Satia struggled to keep up the lie. "He has an army, like I said, and he's very rich. He cares a great deal for me. That's why Septimus was kidnapping me. He was going to ransom me back to my father for money for his dragon hoard." She was rather proud of that detail, and tried to hide the loud thumping of her heart.

"Then he is nothing to me." The wizard puffed out his chest in his armor, leaning back in the throne as if he'd already conquered his enemy without even lifting a hand. "I accept your challenge, princess. Your father's army will be the first I destroy in Takhisis's name . . . but it will not be the last." Thordane's eyes closed for a moment as he imagined his victory. Satia could guess what he was seeing—himself, flying in the air with Nox, hobgoblins, and ogres marching below him, driving into the heart of Ergoth against an enemy destined to kneel before his might.

Satia seized the moment of Thordane's dream of victory, jerking her knife from behind her back and leaping to one side. As she plunged the blade into the neck of one draconian, she saw Septimus leaping onto the other. Satia screamed, "Zargut! Now! *Cut the chain!*"

Zargut had followed her gesture, taking several steps to one side while Satia kept Thordane busy with her lies, but only now did he realize where she'd sent him. He looked back at the wall, staring for the briefest instant at the hook on the wall, the long chain that held the dragon fast to it, and then up at Nox, whose huge body was between Zargut and the throne. The dragon did not flinch, taking in the ogre, his sword, and the hook in a single gaze.

The Ogre King brought the sword of his forefathers down onto the hook with a ringing crash of metal. There was a flash of light, an explosion of magical sparks, and the chain broke in two.

For an instant Thordane stared in horror. Nox's head snapped around, nostrils widening as her jaw gaped open. The mighty wizard raised his hands to cast a spell—but too late. With a bound and a snap of iron teeth, Nox bit him perfectly in half.

CHAPTER EIGHTEEN

Satia stared in blind panic as Nox spat out the corpse of the wizard, shaking her head to get rid of the taste. This was as far as her plan had extended—free the dragon, destroy the Highlord . . . and then it petered off into the land of "and everything will be all right."

But now, faced with a towering, still furious dragon, Satia didn't feel "all right" at all.

Vex and Beset stared in shock, eyes as wide as platters. Nox took one stomping step forward and roared again, her throat working as acid began to burble below her jaws. The two little red dragons squealed, instincts taking over. They scrabbled across the dais, knocking over the throne in their haste as Nox's acid splashed all around them. Vex was the first to launch up into the air, Beset hardly a breath behind. Acid dribbled across their frantically lashing tails, and they yelped in absolute terror. Nox snarled, her wings waving a massive updraft that threatened to knock the Reds out of the air, but they managed to duck over the lip of the roof. Their screams and yelps echoed through the quarry as the two dragons fled in terror.

"I thought dragons were immune to dragonfear?" Satia wondered out loud.

"They are. But angry mother is another thing entirely," Gneech said knowingly. "Nobody immune to that!"

Nox roared in victory as the last of her enemies fled, raising her head and trumpeting so boldly that the rafters shook and dust rained down from cracked wood. Her tail lashed out, pounding against the stone, and her eyes flashed in victory. "Septimus!" She lowered her head to nuzzle her son affectionately. "Remove this collar from around my neck, and we will feast upon these wretched little beasts before we return to our mountain." Her tongue flicked out as though she could already taste Mosango's flesh, and she prowled forward to crouch beside her son.

Septimus looked at her, looked back at Satia and the others, and then back at his mother again. "No."

Nox blinked. "No?" The tip of her tail flicked impatiently. "Remove the collar, son, and I can restore you to your true form. I can't use my magic with it upon me."

Again, Septimus shook his head. "I can't."

Now Nox's impatience turned to anger. "Why not, my son?"

"I can't let you eat them." Septimus colored as though he'd been caught in one of Satia's lies. Nox looked as stunned as Satia felt. Behind her, on the floor of the chamber, she heard Zargut kneeling beside Mosango.

"Will my brother knight live?" Zargut asked hesitantly, watching the goblin's hands press and push at Mosango's wounds.

Gneech twisted a fluffy eyebrow at the ogre. "Brother knight?" When Zargut's only response was a horrible, dark growl, Gneech raised his hands to pacify him. "He fine, he fine. Bit banged up, but at least knows where he is again. Help get him to feet."

Zargut and Gneech lifted Mosango, who stood on legs as weak as a newborn kitten's. Mosango smiled at Zargut. "Well fought, my brother," he coughed, his breath still uneven.

"Well fought indeed," Zargut replied, his hand on Mosango's shoulder.

Nox reached out with a claw and pulled Septimus closer. She tilted her head to the side in order to regard him with one golden eye. "We must kill them all, Septimus." Her voice was low, comfortable, educating him in his duty. "They are beneath us. They cannot leave this place to bear the tale of our humiliation. Do not feel for them, my son. They are as the wind to our earth, a fleeting, passing spirit of no more worth than a puff of air. Takhisis herself cares little for their kind. Let us complete our time here, celebrate our victory, and be free."

"A victory that wouldn't exist if not for their courage," Septimus pressed on boldly. "Mosango fought for us. Satia tricked Thordane into not paying attention to Zargut, and Zargut cut your chain. We owe them." His nose wrinkled and his black eyes flashed. "I don't like owing people."

"Septimus." Nox ruffled his inky hair with a mother's breath. "You are still young, and you do not understand our ways. You have not even yet begun your hoard. You cannot owe these people, and I—I do not even know them. When you are an adult, you will understand, but for now, you do not have the right to stand up for them. Where is your first magic item?" Septimus looked down at his booted feet, clenching his fists against his legs. "You see? Without it, you have not passed the test of ascension into the ranks of the adult dragons."

"Wait." Mosango's voice rang out. "Begging your pardon, ma'am, but I owe your son a debt of thanks." Everyone turned to stare at the old Solamnic Knight, whose failing strength was barely enough to keep him on his feet. "My squire died to your kind. He died because of me. But more, he died doing what he felt was right. And I guess I messed it up afterward, blaming everyone but myself. I was wrong. Your son gave me a chance to make that right, to protect him against a greater evil—an evil that would have restarted the very war that my squire died to end."

Mosango leveled a serious gaze at Septimus. "Take up that armor, son," he said. "It's mine by right, stolen by Thordane's hobgoblins when I was in my cups. It won't fit you—but I figure it's magical enough to start your hoard."

After a shocked pause, Septimus spun on his heel to face his mother again. He crossed his arms and glared up at her. "We don't eat them."

Nox's eyes narrowed. "You are weak. Your time in this human form has lessened you. You will change your mind once you regain your true form. Remove this collar, and then we shall decide."

Reaching out to pat Nox's scaled muzzle, Septimus responded so softly that Satia could barely make out the words. "That might be true. So we're going to make the deal before the collar comes off. I owe these people my life—and yours. It's not a matter of honor, mother, it's a matter of pride." He raised his hand to his lips and whispered, "Besides, if they don't make it out alive, who's going to tell the world what you did to Thordane, and how invincible you are, even chained?"

The dragon laughed, deep and rumbling. Although it was clear that she'd much rather eat them all, she nodded. "Very well. Let these poor fools carry the tale of our power through the land, and tell all of Krynn that the black dragons are not weak in the aftermath of this war. We will not be cowed, and we will not be enslaved." Her golden eyes caught the torchlight like massive suns. "I give you my word . . . on the life of my son."

"Free her," Septimus ordered, pointing to Zargut. The ogre stepped onto the dais hesitantly, holding the sword of his forefathers in sweaty hands. The great ogre looked down at the boy, then sideways at the wall of dragon, and then he gulped. He raised the greatsword slowly and began to wedge it beneath the collar, careful not to cut Nox's shining scales. The dragon lay as still as stone before him.

Zargut turned the sword, placing its edge against the shimmering collar. With a mighty pull, he sawed at the metal, and the blade slid into the metal, pressed by the sheer force of the ogre's strength. Another tug and the sword came free.

The collar fell away from the dragon's neck and

landed on the floor with a loud clang. The shimmering faded from the metal, leaving nothing behind but a molded lump of iron. Nox sniffed it once, and then raised her head to roar once again in victory.

"Thanks, Septimus." Satia took his hand and squeezed it. "I guess maybe evil dragons can be all right."

"No, we can't." Septimus jerked his hand from hers, but paused to give her a wink. "But we can be bargained with."

Nox brushed her nose against Septimus, and Satia took a step back. The tremendous black dragon began to speak words in the Draconic language of magic. A glow, strangely dark and flickering, enveloped Septimus at her command. Satia and the others backed up. Gneech took Satia's arm and put his own around her shoulders. "Is for the best," he said with a chuckle of laughter. "All things must come to an end."

But that didn't stop the tears from gathering in Satia's eyes as the image of the boy wavered and faded away into the smoky cloud. The spell gathered ground, spinning in an unfelt wind as the dragon's voice rose, spreading out to cover a space of ground larger than Zargut, larger than a pony, larger than a house . . .

The smoke faded as quickly as it had come, leaving a dragon in its wake.

He was smaller than his mother, with the same black ridge behind his skull and the same thin, whip-like tail. Rising to his rear legs, Septimus spread his wings and pumped them, bugling in joy at the restoration of his form. His golden eyes flashed and his claws dug into the stone, delighting in his power, and a fresh wash of dragonfear—though less powerful than his mother's—swept around them all. Only Gneech's spell kept them from falling to the ground before him, and Satia decided that was probably what Septimus had been hoping for.

Too bad, Septimus, she thought, and stuck out her tongue.

The little dragon's head was about as big as a horse's, only a third the size of his mother's massive muzzle. But the stare in his eyes was the same—fierce, bold, and utterly unmerciful. "Are you . . . are you ready to go now?" Satia began hesitantly. She couldn't help it if she shrank back a little bit against the goblin's arm.

"No." Septimus snarled, snapping at the air. Satia gasped, trying to stick her courage high and start a fight with him. Had he already forgotten his promise? Was the difference between human form and dragon form as vast as Nox had implied?

Yet even as she opened her mouth to argue, the

dragon Septimus smiled grimly at Satia. His eyes twinkled ruthlessly and his muzzle wrinkled with heartless amusement. "We've got one last thing to do before I take you home."

Epilogue

The sun hovered over the edge of the mud quarries, shining down in weary languor over the goblins of the Howlback tribe as they marched sluggishly up the path toward their dungeon cells. Holg, captain of the hobgoblins, stood on a rough wooden watch-tower at the edge of the broken-looking village. He called down to the still-bruised and battered Dugadee, Urgo, and three other hobgoblin guards, urging them not to spare their whips. "Back to work, you lugs!" he roared at them.

Dugadee shouted from the quarry, "Oi, boss! There's a shadow over the keep tonight!" The squat hobgoblin still had bruises from his failure at the keep. Holg snarled mercilessly.

"S'nothing but the sun behind the rocks. Get them goblins into the keep and get 'em packing mud, or I'll put you on explosives duty in the morning!" Holg cracked his whip over their heads, the sharp popping sound ricocheting off the walls of the quarry.

But the shadow didn't lessen, and even more strangely, it moved in front of the sun. Holg lowered his whip, squinting at the shadow while the hobgoblins lashed the goblins forward. The others didn't seem to notice, paying more attention to the cowering, scuttling goblins than to the wavering sunlight. Holg lowered his whip as he stared up at it, trying to make out the strangely shifting edges. A cold wind blew down from the sunlight, carrying the touch of winter and despair. The hobgoblin shivered despite himself, and lifted his hand to shield his eyes, cursing the sudden shudder in his spine.

They came out of the light like living darkness, the scales of their hides absorbing the rays of the setting sun. Four wings shifted, two vast forms repositioning apart and wheeling like birds of prey stooping to the attack. Holg started to yell a warning, stumbling back on the watchtower's ledge, but the sound caught in his throat at the first touch of dragonfear. It swept over him, colder even than the wind, colder than the realization that there were no more draconians circling the keep's roof, no wizard protecting him from the attack. Holg's heart nearly stopped beating from the fear—and an instant later, he rather wished that it had.

Nox and Septimus hurtled down out of the sky,

claws extended, mouths agape and jetting thick streams of acid down upon the makeshift town. The guards, helpless before the assault, shrieked and were mowed down by their attack. Septimus landed on the watchtower and faced Holg as the shrieks and screams of the others floated up from the quarry. Holg stared up at the smaller dragon with a face as pale as the silver moon, Solinari.

"Remember me?" Septimus hissed, his tongue flicking out.

The rider sitting perched cockily between Septimus's wings leaned forward, placing her elbow on the dragon's shoulder blade. She shook her dark curls, the sun glinting on her soft, caramel-colored features. "I don't think he does, Septimus. You're not half his size anymore."

"No. *He's half mine.*" Septimus drew in a deep breath, prepared to spit out another gush of acid.

Holg yowled in terror and dived off the rickety watchtower, plunging over the edge of the quarry. He fell a good twenty feet and landed with a thick, dumpy splat in the worst of the grayish green muck. Septimus roared a bark of laughter and looked out over the quarry to watch the hobgoblin crawl and whimper for mercy in the mud. Dugadee and Urgo were no better, tied up by the Howlback goblins with their own whips. Meanwhile, Nox gleefully tore apart the village, watching the rest of Thordane's thugs flee screaming into the bog.

Septimus reared back and folded his wings in satisfaction. "That should do it."

Satia looked down at the dancing goblins from his back and saw Gneech run out of the keep's broken doors to be reunited with his kinsmen. Up in the main hall, the ogres were already having a festival of their own, the torches flaring up along the roof and behind the windows of the big chamber with the broken ceiling. The smell of the bog drifted over them, laced with the yelps and yowls of terrified hobgoblins. Every now and then, one would be cut off sharply with a terrible crunching sound.

Nox, after all, hadn't eaten in a while.

"You're sure you don't want to take the armor back to your home first?" Satia asked quietly as they watched the sun set against the horrible cacophony of damage all around them.

"Nah. Mother will take care of that for me. It's not like any of the ogres is going to steal it." They sat there for a while in silence as the clouds turned red with the sunset. The sounds of the goblins laughing and singing echoed against the walls of the quarry, providing a strange counterpoint to the hobgoblin's shrieks of fear. "Anyway, I have to get you home before the prince finds out you're missing," Septimus teased, slapping his tail against the oak beams of the watchtower. It groaned and swayed dangerously under his weight, but the little dragon yawned, unconcerned.

"The prince?"

"Yeah. You know. Your father." When Satia sighed, Septimus burst out laughing. "Without your lying, we never would have gotten Thordane to pay enough attention to us, Zargut wouldn't have made it across the room to cut my mother free, and we'd all be under the thumb of the Highlord of Dirt. Personally, I'm glad you're a liar."

Satia looked out at the goblins dancing on the dirt road. Nox circled the town, her black wings matching the first patches of night to dot the sky in the wake of the setting sun. The ogres in the keep had begun singing a song that sounded archaic, some kind of celebratory battle hymn. Slowly, the young dragon took off from the watchtower. They circled high, Septimus bugling to his mother in farewell before turning south over the bog toward Gwynned—toward home.

Satia thought it over. Lying was wrong. Black dragons were evil, and ogres and goblins were always on the side of the bad guys. And she was going to stop fibbing to everyone, Satia promised herself. It was time to stop thieving, work hard, and become an honest member of society.

"Liar," she smiled at her own thoughts as the sun vanished, the sky now as dark as Septimus's wings.

Laughing, Satia closed her eyes and let the wind rush past.

ABOUT THE AUTHOR

R.D. HENHAM is a scribe in the great library of Palanthas. In the course of transcribing stories of legendary dragons, the author felt a gap existed in the story of the everydragon: ordinary dragons who end up doing extraordinary things. With the help of Sindri Suncatcher and fellow scribes, R.D. has filled that gap with these books.

REE SOESBEE is the author of seven books in the Dragonlance®: The New Adventures series, as well as several other books for children and young adults. She lives in Seattle with the Queen of All Cats and a healthy perspective of her place in the world. She studies both Aikido and Socrates, which leads to interesting internal conversations. You can find her Web site at www.learsfool.com.

ACKNOWLEDGEMENTS

The authors of this book would like to thank Sindri Suncatcher for his excellent introductions and wise words. Further, Ree would like to thank R.D. Henham and Stacy Whitman for their hard work in making this series live.

Ree Soesbee
Assistant to R.D. Henham

**Never start a conversation with a brass dragon—
it might never end!**

Mourning the loss of his parents, orphaned baby brass dragon
Kyani ventures out into the desert to find something to eat,
and finds a gnome named Hector instead.
Hector is not so sure of this little dragon who follows his every
move, until he realizes the hungry brass dragon isn't the only
thing trailing him. He may need the help that only
a fun-loving brass dragon can provide.

Dragon lovers will devour this comical installment in
R.D. Henham's series inspired by *The New York Times* best-seller
A Practical Guide to Dragons.

BRASS
DRAGON CODEX

Coming January 2009